# OLD FLOYD TELLS TALES

The Amazing, Astonishing, Mysterious,
Suspenseful, Dramatic, Tragic, Comic,
Poignant, Pedantic, Enigmatic,
and Almost True Stories of Comstock Miners

by

## R.W. PINGER

NECTAR PRESS
Eugene, Oregon

NECTAR PRESS
nectarpress.or@gmail.com

*Cover photo*: George W. Northrup posing as a gold miner.
© Bettmann/CORBIS, used with permission.

*Cover design*: Jeffrey Duckworth
www.duckofalltrades.com

*Book editng, design & production*: Eva Long
evalong@comcast.net

Typeset in Hoefler Text by Hoefler & Frere-Jones, and
printed in the United States of America.

———————

Publisher's Cataloging-in-Publication

Pinger, R. W. (Robert W.)
    Old Floyd tells tales : the amazing, astonishing,
  mysterious, suspenseful, dramatic, tragic, comic,
  poignant, pedantic, enigmatic, and almost true stories
  of Comstock miners / by R.W. Pinger.
    p. cm.
    ISBN-13: 978-0-9839275-0-1
    ISBN-10: 0-9839275-0-2

    1. Gold miners--Fiction. 2. Short stories, American.
  I. Title.

PS3616.I5655O43 2011          813'.6
                         QBI11-600165

*For Rebecca and Jacob*

*Hain't we got all the fools in town on our side?*
*And ain't that a big enough majority in any town?*

Mark Twain, *The Adventures of Huckleberry Finn*

---

The author's historical note and defense against litigation:

Plenty of the folks mentioned in these stories truly existed. But as near as I can tell, they never did any of the things I say they did. I made it all up. On the other hand, of the folks I write about who never existed, I am telling the full and absolute God's-Own-Truth. I made that up, too. So, if any lawyers are reading this, here is my excuse: I made up the lies about the real people and I made up the truth about the fictional people. That ought to keep us all in court for quite awhile.

*R. W. Pinger*

# CONTENTS

# Blue Dick's Last Night

In 1878 I was working as a pickman at the Northern Belle Mine outside of Candelaria, Nevada. Candelaria was pretty much a new camp, having only been suffering along for a year or so, and did not have near in the way of sophisticated diversion.

It had a couple of saloons of course, the Roaring Gimlet and McKissick's, and a bordello run by a one-legged fat old buss named Gertrude. Naturally we called her Peg, but she never liked the joke much, and she only had but three scrawny girls with bad teeth, so the boys at the mine were always on the lookout for a bit of enriching entertainment.

Now we were just getting off first shift at the Belle when Lightload Harry comes running up to us and says that Blue Dick had got himself shot and killed and was lying on the craps table at McKissick's Saloon with a sheet over his ugly face and his boots poking out the other end.

Well, we could not have been happier if you told us that shit was money because Blue Dick was a man feared from Frisco to Yuma. Dick worked as the collector for John McKissick who allowed the miners to run drinks and some poker on the cuff at his saloon. We could drink all we wanted but John would only permit twenty dollars a month on our gambling draw. I do not know why — it is just the way it was.

Come the first of the month when we were paid, Blue Dick would barge around with a snarly look on his puss and a Model P Colt revolver slung low on his leg in an oily holster. Because of the holster's unctuous condition, the damned Colt was always falling to the floor. That scared us plenty because here was a man who did not know how to properly care for his gun and therefore a man who was capable of unspeakable atrocities.

Some years back Dick had been a turf plunger like the rest of us. Then one day, so the story goes, he left himself in a shaft that was being blasted for a side vein. Besides curdling his disposition, the explosion left his face looking like the innards of a mule's asshole. His wounds were peppered with gunpowder and never healed quite right, having a blackish tint that shone blue in the sunlight. Thus, he got his name that way. All together, Blue Dick gave the impression of a man who fit a nasty job and enjoyed loathsome work.

So when we heard he was resting eternally at McKissick's, we all rushed down there to soak in the spectacle for ourselves. We wanted to make sure it was true, and we all had hopes that a month's worth of vices might somehow vanish from our financial, if not our moral, ledgers. Also, as my friend Kalamazoo pointed out, when you offer the populace something truly worth observing, they will come by the trainload.

I can honestly say that nary a man went to the Roaring Gimlet that night. The whole shift was in McKissick's, leaving no stool unsat on. And there, too, was Blue Dick stretched out on the craps board as advertised.

First thing we did was slip the sheet down a tad to verify the goods. To a man, the gang agreed that Dick looked mighty bad, about the same as he always did. His eyes were wide open and as blank and bloodshot as ever. I would be less than fair to the corpse, however, if I neglected to say that Dick smelled no more rotten than usual. We put the sheet back over his face and felt better for the effort.

Then Twobit Frank got it in his head that even though Dick might not have been the best pal that a poor drunk warthog ever had, the fellow still deserved a genuine first-class funeral same as anybody else. There being no objections to the motion, we commenced to eulogizing the dirtbag as best we could under the circumstances. Most of us had never been within spitting distance of a bonafide church sendoff so we dispensed with the ashes-to-ashes stuff and swung right in to the he-was-always-a-cuss-who-could-hold-his-liquor theme. We were not holding strictly to the swear-on-the-Book-style truth, but it all seemed proper at the time.

In due course, everyone had a say who wanted it and the focus of the audience turned to less morbid concerns. We were drinking and playing cards same as usual, although craps was out owing to the fact that nobody was eager to move Blue Dick's carcass.

I suppose it was fitting when John McKissick shamed us into turning our attention back to the recently deceased one. "Now look here, fellers," he said. "It's all well and good to say those nice things about old Dick here. I'm sure if he could hear you he'd appreciate your kind sentiments."

We gave John a laugh, but only because we thought it might encourage him to say something really funny...which he proceeded to do. "Now this is Blue Dick's stetson I'm holding and I want every one of you mother's mistakes to put a dollar in it so as we can bury Dick proper with a tombstone and something clever carved on it. I'll start it off by putting in five dollars!"

This did not prompt a rush on the box office, but by and by we each coughed up the eight bits, except Frank, who as a matter of principle never paid full price for anything. Frank said, "Ah, John ain't gonna do nothin' with the money 'cept put it back in his own pocket."

"That's a lie!" John declared. "I even figured out the epitaph."

At that he stood up on a chair and put his hand over his heart like he was singing to Old Glory. "He was called Blue Dick because of his head, it was often sick but now it's dead."

We all laughed good at that one, fully understanding that John was referring to some choice comments that Peg had once made about our late friend.

Frank did not hold any grudges, and seeing as how he had only chipped in two bits anyway, he said, "All right, all right. You can pocket the damn money. Just let us get one last look at dick head here."

Frank pulled back the sheet and wouldn't you know that Blue Dick's head snapped up and it roared out, "Whaddaya mean by 'dick head'?"

Frank might have shit his britches right then. I almost did. It was ponderous silent for a moment until John and Dick both start laughing to near die for real this time. Once we got the hang of the humor, we started into a few fine chortles ourselves. Such was the level of what passed for show business in Candelaria that we soon thought this gag was about the best we had ever seen.

Of course, the evening was still young.

Blue Dick rose from the dead and hitched right on to the stetson full of money. "Lookee here what I found," he said, as if surprised. "Mighty generous for a pack of skints like you rascals."

He then plunked the hat on the bar and barked, "Set 'em up for everybody."

Of course you could have knocked us over with a feather duster, not that anyone had one. But we quickly enough sized up the possibilities of the proposition and proceeded to let out the kind of lusty cheer that surely would have awakened Dick even if we had really gone and got himself killed. There was much backslapping and hail-good-fellowing through the next hours as we progressed in slopping up the total of Blue Dick's funeral fund.

Along about midnight it was time for the Northern Belle's second shift to come off work. Anticipating the same bonanza that had blessed the matinee performance, Dick resumed his repose beneath his whiskey-reeking shroud on the craps table and John replaced the empty Stetson by his side. Dick was in the spirit for an encore. The spirits were in him, too.

By this time quite a number of the first-shift boys had pointed themselves in the direction of their tents so they could puke and pass out in privacy. This left a sufficient void in the pews to accommodate the newly proselytized converts of the mine's second shift. The congregation galloped into

McKissick's with the same curious anticipation as the early crowd.

They eyed Blue Dick's big brown brogans peeking silently from the south end, and soon enough, they started mumbling the same sort of nonsense that traditionally accompanies the recently departed. But before McKissick could get off the mark with his tombstone gag, Hal Steiner, a powder man who was not afraid or respectful of much anything, approached the north end of the pantomime and slowly drew down the sheet.

"John? You sure he's dead?" Hal asked.

"Oh, hell yes. Been dead all day. He's as dead as my poor dead pa."

"In that case," Hal said, "your ma might be relieved to know that she ain't a widow no more."

Like slamming a stake in a claim, Blue Dick then let go the most prodigious gust of intestinal wind that Candelaria had ever witnessed, before or since.

What a tour de force! It is hardly likely you will find this kind of grand amusement in the finest theaters of Virginia City or even Frisco. Anyway, the second shift boys appreciated it.

It goes to show what a natural thespian Blue Dick was. He did not give up the act for a single second. He went on playing like he was dead, even though everybody and his dog in McKissick's had figured out the facts of the matter. Then, too, Dick might have just been dead drunk.

No matter. The whole house went along with it. I think we hoped that Dick would grace us with another of his mighty bottom booms.

It was at this juncture, with the festivities starting to lose the interest of the cheap seats, that Lightload Harry danced in and announced that Joe Beans was marching over from the Roaring Gimlet. Joe was Dick's counterpart at the Gimlet and it was well known in our little social circle that you would be ill-advised to invite both boys to the same tea party. Their natural professional rivalry was seasoned by sentiments toward each other best described as homicidal.

It is a wonder Joe had not made his entrance earlier, seeing as how business at the Gimlet must have been something under standing room only. He was probably drunk in a ditch somewhere and had to be found and revived before the reconnaissance could be launched.

Into McKissick's he stomped and we gave him the mute and wary attention of men who are pondering where to hide when the shooting starts. Slowly he walked toward the craps table. Every step of his hobnail boots we could hear on the floor planks. Hell, we could hear every nail tatter on that pine.

Joe stopped at the foot end of the table. He peered at the body with the same disdainful gaze you would give a worm discovered in your whiskey. Nobody knew what to do in the pause that followed. We are only crude miners and are not up to date in the proper etiquette for these occasions.

At last, Hal Steiner stepped up to Joe. Hal placed his hat over his heart and said, "Joe, our dear old friend Blue Dick is no more."

A snotty little smile stole up on Joe's lips, "That worthless clot of pus was lucky to buy it before I had a chance to give it to him. I should have plugged him weeks ago for the good of the camp. Good riddance, dick face!"

And with that he spat a mucus clod into the vicinity of Dick's privates.

Until that spittle pud hit his crotch, Dick had displayed a restraint befitting a dead man. Now, like a vengeful Lazarus, he sprung from his bier with a howl from the depths of hell. With sheet still attached he bounded for the shocked Joe Beans.

Joe may or may not have been a superstitious soul. I cannot say. Perhaps he thought Dick was a ghost. Maybe not. Whether the attack featured a violent haunting or merely Dick's same old mortal corpus, Joe Beans did not linger to inquire. Out the swinging front doors he flew with Blue Dick running a strong second.

Hitting the mud outside in nimble stride and admirable form, Joe turned the race into a steeplechase by jumping the hitching rail. Dick, severely handicapped by the billowing sheet that refused to part the event, almost completed the leap.

We never ascertained if Dick was actually betrayed by sheet or shoe, but the results were clear enough. Only Dick's north end cleared the obstacle. His southern extremities stayed saloon side with his midlands settling squarely on the wooden rail.

If you view the ground as the finish line, the following results could be posted: Blue Dick's Model P Colt won by a nose; Blue Dick's head placed sadly; Blue Dick's torso scratched.

Dick's revolver had departed mid-air from its slippery holster and landed butt down, business end up, and discharged a single round. The slug entered his head below his chin and exited somewhere near his crown. You really could not tell. The going-in hole was clean enough, but the going-out hole took up most all of his scalp. It looked like somebody had taken a pick ax to it.

We carried Dick back into McKissick's and plopped him on the craps table and covered him with the sheet.

Since the night was getting into the mean hours, and because we had all gotten more than our money's worth, most of us had but one or two more drinks before we returned to our tents for the puking and passing out portion of the program.

The next day the craps table was back in use, not too worse for wear, and John McKissick said he was looking for someone to replace Dick, but on no account would he consider hiring that spineless Joe Beans.

I heard they planted Blue Dick up the hill. He never did get a tombstone.

*  *  *

# Goodbye, God.
# We're Goin' to Bodie.

I cannot help but notice that the lode of stories folks tell about their time in the Comstock is more often than not salted with a few shots of the truth. It is an astonishment to me, but miners are generally honorable men and I suppose they feel obligated to color their lies, on occasion, with a crank of accuracy here and there.

What brings this caution to mind is Bodie, California, a camp wedged tight up the arse of Potato Peak just across the Nevada border from Aurora. Most accounts picture Bodie as the rawest, meanest, killingest, and most on'ry camp that ever struck it rich. I will not swear to the truth of these claims for fear of offending all the other contending burgs, but I would be shortchanging you if I did not pass along the local hoodoo.

Time was, the old timers insist, when on every night Bodie had more shootings than fistfights, and more corpses than drunks. The jackass with the job of dragging the stiffs to the cemetery came to know the route by rote and the dumb beast insisted on making the trip three times a day whether it had a payload or not. Even when the traffic in homicide slowed to a crawl, the local denizens could still count on "a man for breakfast," and the fabled "Bad Man from Bodie," so admired by the more imaginative elements of the Eastern press, was in truth any mother's son who managed to greet another dawn. Leastwise, that is what I was told upon arrival in the settlement.

On my part I found the locals to be a gregarious lot prone to blusteriferous blarneyfests administered in generous doses to every unsuspecting newcomer. Although, I will admit their favorite tale tended to contradict the rambunctious nature of the place and pointed instead to their natural pride in thinking that the ol' homestead, despite its rough edges, was a hollerful better than the other hellholes in the region.

It seems that back in the late '70s some fresh-nosed Aurora family was moving their digs to Bodie. Their young daughter, apparently impressed with the wickedness of the destination, wrapped up her evening prayers with the tearful whimper, "Goodbye, God. We're goin' to Bodie."

The story wormed its way into the *Aurora Tribune* and soon enough Aurorans were having a bellyful of gahoots at the expense of their brethren in Bodie. The Bodians, so famous for being quick on the draw, fired back that the poor tyke had been sadly and deliberately misquoted. What the girl had actually said was, "Good! By God, we're goin' to Bodie!"

None of these yarns prove anything, excepting what you want them to, and in that sense I guess they are pretty near the same as mine. I only saw one killing in Bodie. And I will tell you about it.

It was getting into the thaw time of '79 when I arrived in the camp to work at the 'Taint Quite Borrasca Mine. An irksome hack had started smoldering in my chest that winter and I hoped I could get out of the ground and snag a job topland. Hearing that the 'Taint was hiring any bung who could hoist a pick, I left Belleville and landed in Bodie where the 'Taint's chief engineer, Major Crombernobie, hired me as a timber trimmer. The pay is good, you don't lift much, and it is daylight work. So, except for the cough, I was about as happy as I will ever get in this life.

The 'Taint had been a near dry hole for several years until a side passage had nipped into a fat galena vein that paid two thousand dollars to the ton. The managers started hiring quick after that and did not waste their precious time with close inspection of a man's professional qualifications or moral character. By way of being one of the beneficiaries of this enlightened policy, the whole caboodle sat well with me. But not all of the old hands shared my charitable attitude.

William Penrose, the lead driller, was particularly annoyed with the degenerate standards of the new inductees. "Oooo, me darlin' beautays, yer as useful as 'eadless 'ammers," he liked to tell us. We did not always understand Willie's drift because he was from Cornwall, where he had mined tin "from tad to lad to man," so his English was often a vexation and you had to listen carefully to learn if your worth had just been slighted.

The low esteem Willie had for the workers, however, was a love cuddle compared to the vitriol he reserved for the recently appointed mine bull, an itinerant tough named Joe Beans. Among the more genteel descriptions Willie bestowed upon Joe were, "'ell's bloody cur," and "marrow-suckin' corpse bugger." When Willie got into his cups, which was a more than frequent occurrence, he usually referred to Joe as "the dung the devil stuck 'twixt me ivories."

It is beyond me to tell you with any precision what honors these titles conferred, but if you ever heard the hiss of hatred in Willie's voice when he uttered them you would be leaning mighty close to the gist.

The reason for Willie's animosity was clear enough. Joe Beans was hired for one job, that being to prevent the boys from high-grading. I will tell you all about the ins and outs and do's and don'ts of high-grading in some future session. For now, suffice it to say that it is the common custom of allowing a little rich ore to fall into the cuffs of your trousers, or the bottom of your lunch pail, or into your boots or pockets or longjohns, or maybe the specially tailored double-false crown of your hat, before the end of your shift. Miners, by mutual if generally silent consent, regarded the judicious application of the practice as a God-given right akin to life, liberty, and the pursuit of happiness.

We were strongly bent toward that pursuit of happiness clause. Management, on the other hand, tended to view the matter somewhat differently.

Joe Beans took to his bosses' mandates with lip-licking enthusiasm. Ever since the embarrassing demise of Blue Dick in Candelaria, Joe had been aflame with desire to introduce heretofore unimagined miseries to the lives of poor miners. In this ambition he was singularly successful. The managers of the 'Taint, it was rumored, had hired Joe the minute they heard his two guiding principles of labor relations: First, you get 'em flat on the ground. Then, you kick 'em in the head.

Why Joe Beans' high-grading suspicions immediately fell upon Willie Penrose is not for me speculate, but fall upon

Willie they did with a vengeance usually reserved for the Lord Almighty alone. Every day at shift change Joe would ride up to the shafthouse on his lathering sixteen-hand black stallion, Old Scratch, and randomly shake down a digger here and a digger there until Willie emerged.

"Well now, Mr. Penrose," he might say. "How much pinch ore are you toting out today?"

"About yer value in a fair market," was something like Willie would reply.

"Let's count it up then," Joe would snarl. "Strip 'em off."

This command required Willie to get himself buck naked while Joe halted all the other boys as enforced witnesses of the spectacle. From his perch on Old Scratch's saddle Joe would lean down and spear a shirt or vest with a wooden pike and shake the garment in the air.

"Well, Old Scratch, any gold hidden in this rag?" Joe would joyfully ask.

The horse, as if eager to hasten Willie's humiliation, would paw the dirt and snort with contempt. Joe would tug the reins, causing Scratch to shake his head, and the loam of horseflesh would splatter on Willie's bare shoulders. As much as we despised Joe Beans, we soon enough hit on the notion that the damnable stallion was an equal piece of work.

When no trace of ore was evident, Joe would say, "A little light today, Willie. Maybe if you danced a while we'll loosen it up from the dark spot. Jump a bit, Penrose." Then, pointing the pike at Willie's hindquarters, Joe made the driller hop on one foot then the other until mine-bull and horse were satisfied that the high-grading shenanigans at the 'Taint had been foiled for another day.

Given the kowtowing nature of these rituals, a reasonable man might wonder as to why Willie stuck it out at the 'Taint Quite Borrasca Mine. What a reasonable man would have no way of knowing was the best ill-kept secret in Bodie at the time. Willie Penrose was the most adept high-grader in the West. We knew not where he hid it or when he hid it, but the shrewdest minds held that Willie was bagging twenty to fifty dollars' worth of the highest grade per week. Some miners envied him. All of us respected him.

Being a Cornishman, of course, meant that Willie was born to dig holes deep and strong into the earth. Naturally I have never been to Cornwall and I would be hard pressed to point you in its direction, but I and every other backward boobarian knew that when God made the Cornish, He crossed a mole with a mule then added a smidgen of rooster so you could hear the critters burrowing to the bottom. Even management acknowledged the Cornish as pillars of industry and badgered them to entice male relatives large and small to the Nevada goldfields. To this Willie was no exception, not withstanding the painfully obvious suspicion that he was the chief beneficiary of the mine's midnight mudsticking.

Long before Joe Beans had appeared on the scene, Major Crombernobie had prodded Willie into recruiting his Old World relatives for the stampede to Bodie. One of Willie's cousins, a Jack Fenno, had taken the bait and the day came when the 'Taint was to collect this prized enlistee. The Major summoned Willie to his office and for reasons that I was soon to discover, the brass ordered me to report as well.

Upon arrival at headquarters the Major ordered us to have a sit and proceeded to collect his thoughts for three or four minutes while pacing the floor with his hands clasped behind his back. "Men," he finally began. "War is a terrible thing."

If his words strike you as a peculiar introduction to the task at hand, simply keep in mind that Major Crombernobie had served with the 48th Pennsylvania Veteran Volunteer Infantry. You might remember this regiment had tunneled under the Rebels at Petersburg and dynamited them from ditch to damnation. Having survived this debacle relatively intact, the Major fondly regarded the Great Struggle as the most magnificent and glorious event in the history of mankind. All officers of this ilk were prone to frequently reminding us civilians about all that we had missed.

"But the horrors of war are a veritable crucible of duty, honor, and bravery," he continued. "The only thing I ever ask of any of my men is to do their duty honorably and with courage. Do you understand me so far?"

"Yes, sir," we said as one, not having a clue about what the boss was sneaking up on.

"Good. That's good, men. Then I needn't say more?"

"No, sir," we answered, and I bet Willie was thinking the same as me, that saying any more would be a waste on the likes of us.

The Major took the time to mentally review the conversation to date and by-and-by announced, "Good. Good. You're both good men."

He then rolled out a map of California and Nevada on the table. To keep the dern thing from rolling up again he put his Remington revolver on the Pacific Ocean and a bottle of Kentucky Kick on the northern Humbolt River. Satisfied with the structural soundness of the terrain, he started outlining his tactical plan.

He planted a finger a little east of the pistol's trigger guard and said, "This here is San Francisco."

Then he paused so we could look for ourselves. Willie and I peered at his fingernail and nodded sagely to show that besides being brave, honorable and dutiful, we were also attentive and intelligent.

"Our agent there has wired me that the *Pride of Falmouth* has docked. Our man didn't meet the ship, but a J. Fenno from Cornwall was on the passenger manifest. Your cousin Jack, Mister Penrose, has landed in America. If he proceeds per his previous instructions, he will take the Fargo stage to Sacramento and hence to Virginia City, arriving on Saturday. You men will meet him there in the lobby of the International Hotel promptly at two-thirty in the afternoon and immediately escort him back here to Bodie."

The Major lapsed back into silence, only this time his stern eyes were boring into our own. I was getting caught up in the drama of the pageant and started to think that if we failed in our mission the enemies of the union, both foreign and domestic, might yet triumph, and our whole glorious republic would collapse in a heap of something not good ... not good at all.

I swallowed hard and the Major continued, "Under no circumstances are you to frequent the numerous saloons or whorehouses in either Virginia City or Carson City. And heed me carefully, for this is your most crucial franchise. You must not, I repeat not, allow any representatives of any other mine to filch our new employee."

Willie and I sat there for a spell letting the import of the command sink into our skulls.

"Can you do it, men?" the Major asked.

I missed the cue but Willie covered himself with a prompt, "Aye, sir!"

A broad satisfied grin spread over the Major's mug and he slapped Willie on the back. "That's good. Good. Mister Penrose, you may go and prepare yourself."

Willie stood up and left without saluting and I continued to warm my chair while awaiting the other boot to drop. When the door closed the Major picked up his bottle of squirrel whiskey and poured himself a snortful.

"I don't trust that thieving Limey, but we need more good drillers like him," he confided to me. Then he introduced a more personal note to the conversation, "You're a half rank over worthless but at least you're honest. I'm sending Penrose to make sure his cousin gets here and I'm sending you to make sure Penrose gets back. Understand?"

I might have taken umbrage with the remarks if the flattery hadn't been laid on so thick. I managed a mute headshake.

"And I promise you," he promised, "if you don't come back and if both of them don't arrive, I'll have Beans hunt you down, drag you here and ... and ... "

The thought of what Joe Beans would do to me upon retrieval must have been too horrible for even such a grizzled veteran of slaughter as Major Crombernobie. He let the sentence evaporate into his meditations. The madcap mood of the moment disappeared when he smiled and said, "If they both show up fit to work, you'll get a twenty-five dollar bonus."

And on that note of bonhomie I was dismissed.

The next morning Willie and I had ourselves all provisioned for the expedition and piled into the empty lead wagoncar of the Carson-Bodie Freight. Despite our being the honor guard for the treasured Cousin Jack, the 'Taint's management had not seen the necessity of transporting us first class. No stagecoach tickets were proffered. We were traveling "baggage" all the way to Carson City on the twenty-horse jerk line. Once out of Aurora it is about an eighty-mile journey as the crow flies. The trouble was, the Smith Valley Road never did follow the crows, so we braced ourselves heavily in anticipation of the twenty-four hours of bone rattling we were about to endure.

In lieu of the traditional brass band and tearful sweethearts waving hankies, the bon voyage committee consisted of the Major and Joe Beans, the former reiterating his warnings about drinkeries and pleasure palaces and the latter glaring menacingly from atop his beloved Old Scratch. When the shotgun teamster cracked his whip over the team's fannies, Willie and I shouted up a tally-ho and rumbled out of Bodie with the same foolish optimism of General McDowell waltzing the Army of the Potomac into Manassas.

The first leg of the journey proved uneventful. There is not much opportunity for mischief in the bouncing bottom of a freight wagon. Lanterns hung from hames between the teams allowed the rig to drive right through the night and except for the bang-up johnnycakes we ate in Wellington when the horses were changed, nothing worth passing along happened before we pulled into Carson. Milton Sharp, the gentleman bandit, would one day plague the Smith Valley Road but he had not yet introduced his act, and that is another story anyways.

The second leg of our trip also lacked any sparkling anecdotal material. Only by way of giving you your money's worth will I tell you that from Carson City to Virginia City we rode the Virginia and Truckee Railway, twenty-one miles of the crookedest switchback spur ever devised by man. I stopped counting trestles and tunnels after the first ten minutes of the ride but I can swear there were a lot of them. It is a dizzy haul on the V & T and between the twists and turns, the change of altitude, the luxury of sitting on a rail coach bench, the view of mountains and gorge, and the two bottles of nose-paint that Willie and I had consumed on the way, we were both feeling six laps closer to paradise by the time the train tooted to a halt.

Upon getting the boot from the conductor, we set up a temporary bivouac in The Loose Caboose Saloon conveniently located adjacent to the station. Here we laid out our order of battle.

"'Ere's 'ow I sees it," said Willie. "We're 'onour bound ta obey the Major's warnin' agin bars an' 'ores in Virginia City or Carson City. But he din't say nay to anythin' in Gold 'ill which is jist 'cruss the ridge."

Willie, as usual, had all his facts lined up in dress parade and I was not shy to tell him so.

He then cut down to the short hairs. "Soo, 'ere's me plan. We'll snitch up Cousin Jack an' 'ead 'cruss the ridge ta the grandest waterin' 'ole we kin find, then spind the wee 'ars 'tween the satin sheets o' a plump Jezebel or two. What say ya?"

I said, "Wahoo!" and off we headed for the International Hotel.

It was close on four-thirty of Saturday afternoon. If Cousin Jack had arrived at all, we speculated that he would still be waiting in the lobby. After a man, especially a Cornishman, comes halfway around the globe to meet you in a hotel lobby, he is bound to wait a few hours. That is what Willie offered. And that is what I bought. It turned out that we were fully fifty percent right or fifty percent wrong, depending on how you want to view the matter. These things are a little like roulette. You can bet black or you can bet red, but you should never forget there are double-zeros on the wheel, too.

Bodie, or most any other Nevada boomtown, is a pea nugget compared to the glittering mountain that is Virginia City. A typical camp has a mine or two up the slope with the settlement portion tucked in a back pocket. In Virginia City the mines *are* the town, and the smokestacks of a thousand monstrous steam engines crack the landscape like iron forests burning out of control on the crests and flanks of a dozen hills. At the heart of the conflagration is the original Ophir Mine and within a few furlongs lies the California, the Best Belcher, the Sierra Nevada, the Plutus, the Mint, the Scorpion, the Julia, and a hundred more and then some, from the Irving in the north to the Champion in the south, from the Globe Consolidated in the west to the Uncle Sam in the east. It is an awe-striking sight and one I had not soaked in since my regrettable misunderstanding with the 601 Vigilantes back in March of '71.

Creviced between the mines are the saloons, livery stables, assay offices, gunsmiths, dry good stores, bath and barber emporiums, and cathouses necessary to keep the populace in sound mind and starched bib and tucker. Thanks to the thaw, the streets were a royal muck but Willie and I made fair speed past the sundry temptations, past the new Masonic Lodge, past Piper's Opera House, where General Tom Thumb and his wife were appearing, and in due course we sashayed into the lobby of the famous International Hotel.

Right out of the doorframe we saw the establishment was stuffed to its ears with a slippery potpourri of dandy slackers and ruffle-vested bamboozlers. The joint reeked of foo-foo juice, and Major Crombernobie's admonition about fraternizing with strangers shot into my conscience. Some of these mugwumps were pretending to read *The Territorial Enterprise* while they kept one eye on the front portal and one eye on each other. Some of the gents were confabbing around little carved-legged tables and their whiskey glasses rested on tiny lace doilies, if you can imagine that. It did not seem likely we would find a Cornish miner in this cocksure collection of flimflammers, but Willie's keen eyes spotted a heap of matted wool huddled in a corner behind a potted plant and he made straight for it.

Once we had positioned ourselves atower this bundle, an angelic beardless face lifted itself out of the rags and said, "'Ello, Uncle William."

For an awkward while Willie did not say anything at all. Then, sort of sadly, he said, "Oooo, me little lovely, I 'aven't seen ya fer years but er ya 'oo I think ya er?"

By this time even I had figured out that this innocent lad who looked no more than twelve and could not weigh but ninety pounds, was probably not the anticipated granite-armed driller affectionately known as Cousin Jack.

"Aye, sir. I am if ya think me father is Jack Fenno."

"Aye," said Willie and he turned from the boy and blinkingly examined the lobby of the International Hotel as if it had only this second emerged from a pit and into the daylight. When he finished what seemed an inordinately lengthy inspection, he faced the lad and asked, "An' yer father couldn't make it?"

"No, sir."

"An' what name er ya travellin' with?"

The boy thrust his chin out a bit and said, "Jack Fenno, sir."

Willie gave this answer serious consideration before saying, "Aye. Then Jack Fenno ya er. Come along, me darlin' lad, we'll be takin' care o' ya."

We extricated ourselves from the hostel without further incident and as we hiked aimlessly up the street, we all were drinking deeply of our own thoughts, but we were not as yet sharing the bottles. Willie must have been mulling under the weight of his new familial responsibility, while I was calculating if this waif would qualify me for a full share of the bonus promised by the Major. I cannot conjecture about the boy's silent ruminations, but as for me, I determined that because the kid is, after all, a Jack Fenno, I should be eligible for the money ... although a modest discount could be fairly expected.

Willie halted the procession in front of Mrs. Hansen's Scandinavian Beer and Eats. "Me faithful friend, I need some time alone with little Jack," he told me. "Wait 'ere fer us an' we'll collect ya 'fore dark."

Letting the pair out of my sight might have been as prudent as letting a lawyer hold your moneybelt, but I was thirsty and hungry, and the pungy odors of the eatery were a strong incentive to let the wastrels wander where they would. The deal was struck and I willingly turned my patronage to Mrs. Hansen.

The sun was still above the horizon and I had barely dented my meatballs before Willie and Jack returned. Their presence, plus the restoring nature of Mrs. Hansen's brew and victuals, bucked up my inherent trust in the rock-bottom goodness and honesty of mankind. Miner and boy jumped into the repast with hearty relish and before long we were as jolly as the first arrivers at a G. A. R. reunion.

The tale Jack told was a gripping one, not unlike the more literary works occasionally offered on the boards of Piper's Opera House. A cave-in had claimed the life of his father, the real Cousin Jack Fenno as it were, and because the lad's mother had already died of consumption some years before, Fenno fils was left an orphan in a cruel and heartless world. Shortly before the tragic accident, Fenno pere had spent his last farthing on passage to California. His plan was to send for his only child after making a quick fortune in America. The relatives who housed the lad in the interim would be generously rewarded for their trouble. Alas, twelve tons of runaway tin ore had put a bash on the dream. The penniless Fenno tribe in Cornwall could hardly be expected to feed another mouth without hope of compensation, so they encouraged the boy to exploit his only asset, the pre-paid booking on the *Pride of Falmouth* bound for San Francisco, and place his fate in the hands of his father's loyal cousin, dear old he-should-be-rich-as-Midas-by-now "Uncle" William Penrose. Little Jack had read the letter calling for a rendezvous in the International Hotel, so this steadfast urchin (whose christened name was omitted from the narrative) packed his meager belongings in a thread-worn carpetbag and bravely set out for his El Dorado.

Willie seemed familiar with Act One of the melodrama, but the opening of Act Two kindled an edge of the seat interest. "An' 'ow, me 'andsome boy, did ya git yerself from Frisco ta Virginia City?" he asked.

"Ooo, I 'ad a bit o'luck on that account. I met a young gentleman an' wouldn't ya know, 'e's an orphan too, an' 'e too was goin' ta Virginia City, an' 'e lent me the money fer the trip."

I was not in the least amazed that a handy coincidence introduced itself into the plot, but Willie must never have seen a play at Piper's. He was astonished with this development and shot a volley of questions at the boy, "What young man? What did 'e want from ya? 'Ow are ya supposed ta repay 'im?"

Jack was taken back by the anxious urgency of the queries. He looked to me as if expecting help and finding no answers he mumbled, "Well, Uncle, 'e's only a nice boy. I don't know much. 'Is name is James Buchanan Adams an' 'e's an orphan too. An' 'e's lookin' for a man named Joe Beans in Virginia City. 'E said I could pay 'im when I could, or never. 'E din't care.

"Joe Beans!" Willie thundered.

I will forgive you if you think the Joe Beans angle is hard to swallow. Even the management of Piper's might find this one difficult to shove off on their public. I can only hide behind the fact that the boy said what he said and now I am telling you about it. Though the words came from the mouth of a mere babe, Willie found them rough going down.

"Joe Beans," he moaned. "This is trouble, me boy. I ken't fathom why any sane man would want the company o' Joe Beans."

"'E din't tell me, Uncle. Did I do wrong?"

"Did you?" Willie asked.

"No, uncle. I din't. I swear."

"No wrong at all?"

"None."

The conversation had taken a direction that was getting out of my depth. The Cornish, I concluded, were simply enigmatic by virtue of birth and mother tongue.

Willie weighed the boy's words then said, "I believe ya. But I'm nagged 'bout the matter. 'Tis clear we need ta repay yer debt. Me kin ken't start in the 'ole. But a man lookin' fer Joe Beans ... " He shook his head. "What do ya make o' it?" he asked me.

I was pleased to be privy to the Fenno/Penrose family council and jumped in with a few well-chosen observations. Just because the fellow sought the congress of the infamous Beans, it did not necessary follow that the man was a scoundrel, although I admitted it was not exactly a chip in his pot. Perhaps he was serving in some official capacity, preferably from the county sheriff's office. Or maybe he was attempting to collect a debt. After all, the evidence pointed to this Adams character being rather quick and easy with his loans.

Willie perked up a measureful. "I 'adn't looked at it from those bents. Aye. There could be a profit in it. It could be a 'andsome profit. It might even be the 'eavenly 'and of divine retribution. Aye, we might bist find yer Mister Adams, lad."

"Oooo, that would be grand, Uncle," Jack said. Then hastily added, "Because I wouldn't want ta be be'oldin' to any man."

I cheerfully contributed that Willie might also want to thank the fellow for safely shepherding Little Jack to Virginia City.

"Nay, I doubt I'd go as far as all that," he grumbled.

As I have already related, the Cornish are an odd race.

We had filled our bellies and unanimously passed the resolution to dredge up James Buchanan Adams, if we could, and seeing as how there was no more new or old business on the agenda we settled accounts with Mrs. Hansen and launched our enterprise without further debate.

I had long since abandoned the vision of a night's drunken revelry and cavorting between satin sheets with a plump Jezebel. Willie and I had not spoken further on the subject but, following the discovery of our young charge, the notes played in The Loose Caboose were clearly out of key with the harmony of our newly formed trio. Our song now was "Onward Christian Soldiers," and we three stoutly marched pure of heart and noble of spirit into the mud-begobbed streets of Virginia City.

When the Crusaders first rolled into The Holy Land they were more than likely favorably impressed with the place. It is much the same with the silver city of Nevada.

In fairness to the metropolis, I initially gave you a pretty picture with the town's shirt studs all showing and its trousers fly neatly buttoned up. But just like the Crusaders who probably discovered Jerusalem's finest hotels had bedbugs, a night tour of Virginia City could convince you that the town closely resembles a two-hole outhouse built on a beehive. Beneath the high style and luxury lies ample opportunity for being stung on the backside.

Willie knew this as well as I did, so it followed that our search for Mr. Adams started with our cards tucked snugly to our chests. We would approach a likely waterhole and Willie would remain outside with Jack. I would enter the establishment, pay for a rye and water at the bar, then casual-like ask the barkeep, "Say, partner, has Jimmy Adams been in here tonight?"

The barkeep would then say, "Wawl, can't say as I know ol' Jimmy. What's the cuss look like?"

I would then give the brief description provided by Jack, and the drinkman would say, "Naw, don't think he's been in."

At this juncture in the banter I'd throw in the flourish that the cuss was probably inquiring about the whereabouts of our dear ol' chum, Joe Beans.

The fellow would scratch his head and say, "Naw, nobody's asked about ol' Joe lately, but if I see either one of them, who should I say wants to know?"

That is when I would push two bits worth of Willie's high-grade across the bar and say, "I'll come back later and see if Jimmy's made your acquaintance."

Willie thought this approach would do justice to a pack of Pinkerton's best, but it did not bring us early results and after the tenth rye and water my capacity to analyze the intelligence was dulling some. Willie prudently suggested we switch roles for a time and he conducted the interviews while Jack was kept occupied propping me up on the street. Willie's inquiries proved no more fruitful than my own and although his capacity for rye and water was admirable, by midnight we agreed on an entirely different dodge. Willie and I snoozed on the boardwalk while Jack snuck into the saloons and determined by eyeball if James Buchanan Adams was on the premises. This clever wile soon hit pay dirt.

Willie and I were resting in the eaves of the Whiskey Trust Saloon when Jack scampered out of the joint and excitedly announced, "'E's in there. It's 'im. Now what do we do, Uncle?"

The glad discovery of our prey at a time when our energies were rapidly flagging was just the tonic to clear Willie's head and focus his thoughts on treeing the varmint. "Fine bit o'work, me lad," he said. "Now ya point 'im out an' leave the rist ta me, fer I want me own words with the man."

As Willie stood and kicked the mud from his boots, a young man dressed in an ankle-long duster and carrying a back-knap and spit new Winchester repeating rifle emerged from the Whiskey Trust and purposefully trod into the street without giving notice or glance to our posse assembled on the boardwalk.

"That's 'im, Uncle!" Jack cried and yanked Willie into the chase. In a wink we three whipped ourselves from standstill to a splattered canter, but our quarry was a spry colt and was steadily putting the winning lengths between himself and the pack. On a dry course we might have yet nosed him out. On the sloppy track, and with Willie and me still a wee sloppy ourselves, the race looked like a no-contest. Jack, bless his quick-witted little head, brought the stampede to a merciful halt by calling out, "Jimmy! Jimmy! Wait. It's Jack! I foun' me Uncle!"

The leader reined himself in. His now breathless pursuers closed the gap to a dead heat and were rewarded with a warm enough welcome. "Jack! Whoa! My little pal! It's no hour for you to be out on the streets."

"This is me Uncle William. 'E wants ta repay yer kindness ta me," answered Jack.

"Aye," Willie gasped. "We've mebee business. Only ... I kin nay think or talk if I'm pantin' in the sludge."

Willie sensibly gestured back in the direction of the Whiskey Trust but this wordless request for moving the convention's venue met with reluctance on James Adams' part.

"That's good of you, sir. And I'll gladly accept your compensation on another day. But tonight I have business of my own and I mean to get about it."

"It's 'bout Joe Beans I want ta ask ya," Willie replied. Jimmy's breezy young-gent-about-the-town pose dropped like a dove in a skeet shoot. His eyebrows hunkered to a meeting on the bridge of his nose and his jaw clinched so tightly and abruptly that I could almost hear the crunch of his teeth. His words became coldly measured, "You know where I can find Joe Beans?"

"Mebee," Willie said and pointed again toward the Trust.

Much to my relief, for I was beginning to feel the dampness swell into my chest, a stiff wisp of a head dip from Jimmy signaled his consent and we re-trekked our way to the aforementioned oasis. The backroom was near empty and dark and quiet, so after laying claim to a table and rounding up three manly ales, and a vanilla fizz for Jack, the negotiations commenced in a properly conspiratorial setting.

James Buchanan Adams was a fine looking youngster once he removed his hat and duster and set aside his Winchester repeating rifle. Nineteen years of age he was by his account. He had dark thick hair, a nose that fit his face, clear blue eyes, clean skin, flat gut, and in most other characteristics looked nothing much like Willie and me. He was already taller than us, too. And you could tell by his loosey-goosey frame that he still had growing to do. He could also look a man square in the eye, which is not a common trait among most youngsters, or most elders, come to think about it.

Willie exercised the host's prerogative and introduced the first topic of conversation for the evening. "'Ow much do I owe ya fer Jack's travel?" he asked.

"Seventeen dollars will do it," said Jimmy.

"Will ya take greenbacks or do ya want gold?"

"I'm at your convenience, sir."

Willie opened his shirt and from below table level he unbuttoned his body bank and counted out a stack of bills.

Placing the mound on the table, he said "'Ere's seventeen dollars an' two fer yer interest."

Jimmy picked up the money and counted out seventeen bills. The remaining two he pushed back toward Willie. "It's seventeen I loaned, sir, and it's seventeen I'll collect."

Willie slowly nodded his head in approval and returned the two dollars to their nest. Jimmy waited for Willie to close the shirt before asking, "Are you a friend of Joe Beans?"

"Mebee," said Willie. "What brings ya ta look fer the man?"

"I'm looking to find him. Do you know where he might be?"

"I might. It could depend on yer business."

Jimmy sniffed the bait for a moment but did not bite. "I mean you no harm, sir. And I admire your nephew. Jack's a spunky and brave boy. It's not easy or right for a little one to make his way without a father. A mother can only do so much, even if she dies in the effort. A boy must have his father."

If Jimmy had a noticeable fault, it was this somber and serious way he had of looking at matters. By all that is natural, a lad that age should be brimming with pranks and larks and abuzz with the idea of giving life a hotfoot. Jimmy had all the ho-ho rib-poking puckishness of an undertaker on a rainy day.

"My business is my business, sir," he told Willie firmly. "What say you to this? I'll pay your price for your help, if it leads me to Joe Beans."

It sounded like a called hand to Willie, so he finally laid his cards on the table. "'Ere's where I be, lad. If yer business is o' any good ta Joe Beans, y'll git nay 'elp from William Penrose. If yer business is ta blow an ill wind at Joe, then I be yer man. I'll lead ya ta 'im. What say ya?"

"I can't judge if my business is for the betterment or detriment of Joe Beans. That's for others, or for God, to decide," Jimmy declared. "You see, sir, I aim to kill him."

Willie's eyes widened. Little Jack began to softly cry. I took a deep swig on my ale and thought, ain't this a pisser!

Jimmy said to Jack, "Don't you cry for me, little man. There ain't enough tears even for yourself. I'm ready to do what I must do or die trying."

This counsel was not comfort to Jack who started blubbering seriously and had to wipe his nose on the sleeve of his shirt.

"'Ere, boy," said Willie, handing Jack a bandanna and a look of admonishment which I considered sterner than necessary. Willie then leaned his chair onto its back legs, plopped his muddy boots on the table and smiled.

"Aye," he said to Jimmy. "Ya've knocked on the proper church door, James Adams. We'll deliver ya ta yer fate. The only price y'll pay is tellin' me 'ow ya came 'bout ta be on yer noble task."

Jimmy proved to be an adequate narrator, requiring only semi-occasional prodding and questions from his audience, and fewer fresh ales to tell his story than Willie and I required to hear it.

He was born in San Francisco to Susanna Shea Adams and Andrew Jackson Adams early in the year of 1860. Andrew worked as a cooper and Jimmy's mother could point to the barrels in their house and say, "Your daddy made these."

The memories of his father were faint because the old man apparently worked night and day and did not hang about the house too often. Despite this industriousness the family was poorer than swamp water, and financial matters took a turn for the worse on December 23, 1871, when Andrew Jackson Adams disappeared. "I think the Bay just swallered him up," was how Susanna Adams explained the absence to her son.

After that, she never mentioned Andrew again, other than to repeat that the Bay just swallered him up, and she forbade the boy to ever mention their loss. She never remarried, and having to depend on her pitiful income as a Russian Hill washerwoman made life hard for them. As Jimmy grew older, his mother grew more frail. More frequently she was too weak to climb the hill to the mansions of her employment and Jimmy had to forego schooling and work in her stead. Eventually she could not work at all and the boy assumed full support of the family by selling rags and papers and running errands for the Barbary Coast barroom proprietors.

This was the state of affairs until March of '78, when Susanna Adams was stricken with a last fever. After her funeral Jimmy felt freed from his order of silence and vowed in the name of his sainted mother that he would uncover the mystery of the long lost Andrew Adams.

From that day on, he asked one and all of his wharfside cronies if they knew anything about his vanished pa. Either they did not know or they would not say, and for many months the book remained closed on his father's sudden departure.

Then Jimmy met up with an honorable barkeep named Spuds Halligan, and he found all he needed to know about his father's sad end. Andrew Jackson Adams was killed off, Spuds testified. Spuds claimed he was only providing this information so Jimmy could mourn properly and let the matter rest.

But Jimmy could not let it rest and he nagged Spuds to identify the murderer. It was a man claiming the name of Joe Beans, Spuds reluctantly admitted. Joe had stood at the bar and confessed he killed Andy to put him out of his misery. For reasons that stumped Spuds, Joe claimed that Andy's death would allow Joe to flee to Nevada where he hoped to make a fortune. Plenty of Andy's friends had witnessed Joe's confession, but it had occurred a long time ago, and even when it happened nobody thought it was any of their business.

What Joe did to Andy was, according to Spuds, for Joe's conscience and Christ almighty to settle. Jimmy could not accept the laissez-faire of Andrew's former friends. He swore that only murderous revenge could balance the ledger for the loss of his father.

By working nearly around the clock for a year and selling his mother's tattered possessions, he accumulated more than enough money to purchase his Winchester rifle and finance the trip east. He would not be deterred until he found and killed this Joe Beans, even if it meant shaking Nevada by its heels until its fillings dropped out. So here he was, and the Almighty must be on his side because he had picked up Joe's trail on the very first night.

Lastly, he wanted us to know that he had not before breathed a word about any of this to anyone, not even his little friend, Jack, because he did not want Joe to get wind of the chase, and he would appreciate it if we kept our mouths shut, too.

As a tear-jerking tale it topped Little Jack Fenno's by a fistful. Willie and I did not stand on our chairs and yell "encore" when the curtain fell, but we were deeply moved by the saga and greatly respected the sincerity and intrepidness of our young Mr. Adams.

Jack was enthralled. His initial whimpering had given way to a chin-in-his-hands gaze of undying admiration. Or maybe the little scrapper was just suffering from fatigue and too much vanilla fizz.

If it strikes you that my errand to Virginia City had bogged down in a glutted market of orphans, I should remind you that folks were plenty more eager to meet their Maker back in those days, and naturally this created a surplus of parentless waifs to bump against us Nevada miners. Willie and I give nary a thought to the unlikiness of looking for a Cornish driller and digging up a couple of foundlings. Like I said, there are always those double-zeros on the wheel.

By this time of the night the Whiskey Trust was empty except for us and the bartender, who was snoozing in a chair next to the billiard table. It had been an eventful enough day. We closed the store and wandered into the streets wondering where we might rest our tuckered heads. Jimmy said he had passed a place called Ma's Beds and Bunks that advertised a night's sleep for twenty-five cents, sheets included. He led us to the establishment which in a previous life had been a mule train stable. When Willie saw that was only one cavernous room lined with rows of log-sawing diggers, he turned up his nose and downed his thumb.

"We'll nay be beddin' in a Lan's En' flop'ouse," he said. I could not guess why Willie got so fussy. Many were the nights in Bodie when he and I had dreamt our dreams from a ditch. Ma's Beds hardly offered the sleek joy of a Jezebel's, but it was swept and dry and I did not notice any vermin crawling about.

"I'll be payin' fer proper rooms in a respectable 'otel tanight," he told us. So we followed him until he found a two story white-washed frame structure with a large sign proudly proclaiming itself the location of Millard's Hotel for Traveling Agents — Peddlers and Drummers Welcome. This hospice met with his approval and although we were not claiming membership in the honorable order of hucksters, Millard gladly accepted two of Willie's dollars in exchange for two room keys.

Jimmy wanted to pay his full share of the tariff but Willie insisted that he was responsible for the upgrade in accommodations, so the tab was his alone to bear. A filibuster was avoided when Willie accepted Jimmy's offer to contribute two-bits toward the total. For my part, I welcomed Willie's generosity without comment. As my old friend Kalamazoo used to say, reasonable parties can always reach agreement if one of them is willing to surrender.

The room Jimmy and I shared had a big brass double bed, a round table, two wooden cane chairs, and hanging on a wall was a framed picture of upper-crust Yankees taking a sleigh ride. I supposed Willie and Jack's room down the hall looked about the same. While Jimmy was getting down to his longjohns I went out back to do my duties, and upon returning I found

Willie in our room. "Ta tired ta sleep," was his explanation. "I thought I'd see in on yerselves."

Jimmy said, "Suit yourself," then climbed into the bed and promptly knocked off.

Willie sat himself on a chair and started talking half to me and half to the table leg about the old days in Cornwall when he and Cousin Jack used to play draughts at the local pub and generally raise hell around their village. The last I remember about the night I was lying under the quilt next to Jimmy, and Willie was rattling on about black treacle and porridge, or some other such nonsense.

Come the dawn I awoke to find Jimmy slumbering blissfully at my side, and Willie, fully clothed, asleep on the floor and snoring like a sailor. Anyone who thinks the Chinese are inscrutable, just has not met a Cornishman.

The Saturday morning that greeted us was crisp and brightish. A good day for travel, and we were traveling light. Willie and I had the clothes we wore. Jack had topcoat and carpetbag. And Jimmy carried only his back-knap and the Winchester. Virginia City was sleeping off its sins of the previous night, so our competition for breakfast at Mrs. Hansen's and for tickets at the V & T station was slim. By noon we were cradled in the rocking arms of a railcar and, by God, we were goin' to Bodie.

A good night's sleep, a rib-sticking breakfast, and riding through the most beautiful country this side of Eden generally bucks up the disposition of man and boy. Jack and Jimmy and Willie all seemed perky as teakettles. They were whistling at the waterfalls and marveling at the mountaintops and all together acting like puppies at a picnic.

I was not exactly a Mr. Gloomgates myself, but thoughts of the Reckoning Day were itching my mind. Jimmy was going to kill Joe Beans. So far, so good. But a prudent man considers all the horses before he buys. Joe Beans might object to the bargain and introduce a few clicks and cackles of his own. He might kill Jimmy Adams. Not so good. Either way, somebody would probably wake up old Marshall Higgins and prod him over to Bodie to arrest the survivor. In a subsequent trial, either potential defendant could make a reasonable case. Joe could claim self-defense. Jimmy could tell his woeful saga and plea justifiable homicide. If the judge or jury were not bribed, and that is usually a fifty-fifty proposition, either defendant would get the walk-free verdict and all the boys in town would sleep easier knowing civilized Western justice had once again triumphed. Or, and this was another horse, the good citizens of Bodie might get tanked up and lynch Joe before Higgins doddered into town. Or, Major Crombernobie might have Jimmy dragged before a firing squad and shot at dawn as an example to the rest of us.

No matter what happened, the management of the 'Taint Quite Borrasca Mine was most likely to perceive the episode as an inconvenience. I could not help worrying about the extent to which the Major would hold me personally responsible. So, while Willie and Jack and Jimmy frolicked in the aisle of our V & T railcar, I tended to brood.

In Carson City we had to layover for the night because the Smith Valley stagecoach to Aurora and Bodie only ran on Mondays and Wednesdays and even then only if it had six passengers. No more jerk line freights for us. Willie was bankrolling our expedition in Nob Hill fashion. In that vein he put us up in the Carson City Commercial and Residential Boarding House, a posh joint that besides double brass bed and round table and wooden chairs, had two framed pictures hung in each room.

Jimmy spent the afternoon practicing with his Winchester repeating rifle. He shattered the life out of a few dozen empty gin bottles and when satisfied that his eye was sharp and his was finger steady, he took to instructing Jack in the use of the weapon. I could tell that Willie was none too happy about this, but he did not voice complaint. Jack was as frisky as a tadpole and his constant laughing and gay peppiness were a big hit with Jimmy but eventually got me to wondering if the boy was a bit daft.

We turned in early that night, using the same formula for room assignments that had served us well in Virginia City. And darned if Willie did not show up again to ply lullabies on Jimmy and me. And darned if he did not again spend the night sleeping on our floor. Here was a man forking over hard pilfered gold for a soft bed, then opting to take his repose like an Arkansas coon hound. Any sign of daftness on Little Jack's part could be readily explained; the trait apparently was rooted in the family tree.

With the Monday morn we boarded the stagecoach bound for Aurora. The opportunity amongst ourselves for light banter or confessional soul-searching was dampened considerably by the added presence of Misters Ephraim Kupperkeeper and

Solomon Gould. Kupperkeeper sold tunnel track and Gould sold hand tools, or maybe it was the other way around. These two hawkers were both hightailing to Aurora where they hoped to tote up big orders from the Esmeralda Mines before putting the pitch on the 'Taint's management. They started yakkin' in Carson and found themselves so fascinating that they never did give it a rest. Kupperkeeper would get busy regaling us with how he personally led Henry Comstock to the Ophir Mine site, then Gould would let slip that the Ophir was nothing but a piss rut until he encouraged George Hearst to elbow in on the deal. There was not a single mine or millionaire in Nevada or California that these fellows had not given a shove in the right direction, and we heard about them all. I am amazed that the mass of historical insight, mechanical expertise, and sharp financial acumen these gasbags blew into our coach did not send the whole rig airborne. Wagon and horses managed to stay earthbound and we rolled into Wellington at sunset.

This was our last night before we would reach Bodie. Wellington is not much more than a puddle in the sand, so the accommodations are more of the style to which I am accustomed. Kupperkeeper, Gould, Willie, Jimmy, and I all slept in chairs leaned against the depot shack walls. The station manager's wife, she of the manna-like johnnycakes, took pity on Little Jack and slept him in her cabin away from the corrals. The boy must have awakened the old gal's maternal instincts, because the next morning she was licking his fur like ma cat and kitten, and spooning the flapjacks down his gullet with extra syrup. All the while she was giving the rest of us the evil eye and hammering Willie's ears with the notion that eventually he must "set things right" for the child. Willie accepted this henpecking with a meekness that disgusted me at the time. Soon enough, of course, everything would make sense.

Late on Tuesday afternoon we rattled into Aurora, stopped briefly to let Kupperkeeper and Gould float into Glasscock's Saloon, then proceeded to Bodie in a tensely blessed silence. Willie spent the time in frowned contemplation of the chaparral. Jimmy did nothing save stroke his Winchester with an oilcloth until barrel and stock shone like a mintbar. Jack never let his eyes loose from Jimmy, and I resumed speculating on my chances for bonus or banishment at the whims of Major Crombernobie. By the time we set foot to Bodie's terra cognita we were a melancholy lot.

It was no disappointment to me that neither Joe Beans nor Major Crombernobie were on muster to welcome the stagecoach, for I was not eager to witness the denouement with empty stomach or dry throat. Joe and Old Scratch were probably up at the shafthouse sweating gold dust out of the day shift boys, and the Major must have been barricaded in his office reviewing the Siege of Petersburg.

A few of the night shift boys were gathered to see if the stage might exgorge a package of cookies from mother or a new "laundress." When only we four emerged, and the mail pouch produced only official-looking correspondence for the 'Taint's management, the men waved a disappointed greeting to Willie and me and shuffled away for a last pipe and drink before work start.

Jimmy coolly eyed the dispersing crowd and whispered to Willie, "Is he in this bunch?"

"Nay, son," Willie whispered back. "'E'll be the one with pus in his eyes and ridin' a flame snortin' black 'orse."

"Well then, let's go find him and get the deed done."

"Oooo, not sa 'asty, lad. I been givin' the matter me attention en I'm thinkin' ya might be wisest ta sneak up on the task, as it were."

"No," said Jimmy. "I didn't come this far to act like a coward."

"It ain't cowardice, I'm thinkin," Willie counselled. "It's more on the line o' prudence."

Jimmy looked straight at Willie and said, "Thank you, sir. No. I am here to kill the man who killed my father. Let's be done with this business."

The hardrock resolve in his voice sent a shiver through Little Jack. The boy clutched my arm. I wanted to reassure the youngster, toughen him if I could, but something in the warm desperation of his grip stayed my tongue and I could not utter a word. The fact is, I was embarrassed about the scene. At the same time I felt happy and a little sweaty and I allowed Jack to remain knotted on my elbow.

We were still standing in the middle of the road. The stagecoach was gone. The miners were gone. Jimmy was still looking silently into Willie, like a cocked gun waiting for a trigger squeeze.

"Yer a stout man, me James Buchanan Adams," said Willie. "I nay want ta see ya dead."

"I need do it in my own way," said Jimmy. "I need to do it now."

"Aye," Willie said sadly. He picked up Jimmy's back-knap and walked away from the town toward the 'Taint Quite Borrasca Mine. Jimmy followed him with Winchester tightly in grip. I latched onto Jack's carpetbag using the only free arm I had, and with Jack entwined on my other arm like a dwarfed Siamese twin, we trudged up the hill for the showdown.

By this time of day the toplanders of the morning shift were drifting down from their toils and they eyed our parade with amused curiosity. We said nothing to them, but they must have sensed that a tedium-relieving occurrence could be in the offing because quite a few of the boys turned themselves around and trailed us toward the mine. The higher up Potato Peak we marched, the more miners we encountered and the larger our company grew. Jack was giving the tear ducts a pretty good workout by now and since my bandanna was a snot-grimey affair I let him slobber all he wanted on the chest of my waistcoat.

We were closely approaching the 'Taint's shafthouse when we saw the man riding down the hill. Silhouetted against the dusky skyline, Joe Beans and Old Scratch loomed as black and relentless as a Kansas thunderhead.

When he spied the approaching mob Joe slowed Scratch to a walk, tucked the tail of his frock coat behind his holster, cocked the revolver's hammer, and leaned forward in the saddle. The pike that previously served as a Willie-prodder was now perched cavalry fashion in Joe's left hand and arm, and Lucifer's own lance could not have looked more lethal. Joe's right hand slip-tied the reins around the saddle horn and he directed Old Scratch by touch of boot-toes and spurs. Man and horse were as one, as indivisible as snake and fangs.

Willie stopped, placed a hand on Jimmy's shoulder, and spoke quietly. "There 'e be, son. Don't be makin' any noble gestures. Don't be doin' any grandstandin'. Take aim 'fore 'e's in pistol distance an' shoot first. If ya miss, shoot agin and keep shootin' 'till ya get 'im, or ... well, jist keep shootin'."

"I've done this a thousand times in my dreams, sir. I know what I'll do, and I know how I'll do it."

"Jist shoot first!" said Willie. "God be with ya."

"Aye, sir," said Jimmy and he walked alone toward the menace coming slowly and surly down the mountain.

The miners had all figured out that real excitement was in store. They took their seats beside the road on those rocks that looked safely out of bullet range. If they had been given advance notice of the contest a lively betting book would have undoubtedly been under way. As it was, the boys could only take in the spectacle for its entertainment value and their sporting instincts would have to await satisfaction on another day.

Little Jack remained a weeping bundle on my person and Willie positioned himself as a shield between child and action. It was high drama indeed, and far more suspenseful than that night in McKissock's when Joe confronted Blue Dick's fake corpse.

Up the mountain walked James Buchanan Adams. Down the mountain came Joe Beans and Old Scratch.

Some fifty yards from where we stood, Jimmy halted. Joe stopped Old Scratch about twenty yards from Jimmy. Because we were downwind of center stage, the words of the principals punched loud as powder sticks.

"Are you Joe Beans?" Jimmy asked.

"That's me, boy. Better say what you have to say, right now. I'll be soon riding over that place you're standing in," Joe answered.

Jimmy responded, "Did you know a man named Andrew Jackson Adams?"

Unlike Joe's usual inclination toward quick and snide retorts, he said nothing, choosing to squint his eyes and examine his adversary more closely.

"Did you murder Andrew Adams in San Francisco?" Jimmy demanded.

"Who are you?" shouted Joe.

"James Adams. And I have a debt to repay." With those words Jimmy raised his rifle, too hastily aimed it at Joe's bean, and fired off a round.

The bullet must have flown high or wide by a rod or so, but close enough that Old Scratch reared in terror. Joe kept saddle, but instead of firing back or charging the lad at pike point, he screamed out, "No, boy! No!"

Jimmy cranked the Winchester lever and fired another shot, no more accurate than the first. This second discharge effectively brought the conversation to a close. Joe reined Scratch into a sharp wheel-about and spurred the horse into a gallop back up the hill. Jimmy futilely gave chase, cranking and firing at the rapidly retreating Beans until the five remaining cartridges of the repeating rifle were spent into the uncaring skin of Potato Peak's face.

To a man the miners sent up a glorious cheer. Then they took to laughing because the notion of a lone kid routing the much-feared Joe Beans was just too funny for serious contemplation. Most of them had heard the Davey and Goliath yarn, but few of them believed in it. Until now.

Lightload Harry accurately caught the mood of the gang when he shouted out, "Three cheers for the new boy!" And while the boys were hip-hip-hurrahing, they did not notice that Little Jack had broken from my arm and was running whampgush for gully toward our freshly laurelled young hero.

It was fortunate that nobody except Willie and me were paying critical heed because Jack wrapped his arms around Jimmy's neck and said, "I love ya, Jimmy! I love ya with all me heart!" Then Jack kissed Jimmy flat on the lips and would have smothered all the rest of his face with sloppy smooches if Jimmy had not pulled himself away and turned his back in red-faced shock.

"Oooo, me fragile little flower," Willie said to no one in particular. To me, he said, "Don't ya be thinkin' what yer thinkin'!"

"M ... me?" I stuttered, "I'm not thinking anything at all." But the truth was I was seriously weighing the possibility that there was more to Little Jack's daftness than first met the eye.

"Keep yer yap shut an' stick ta me side," Willie commanded.

After we had gathered up Jack and Jimmy and begged off all the boys who wanted to celebrate the gunfight by buying us drinks, we retired to Willie's cabin where the truth came out in a dam burst.

Willie swore me to secrecy and explained that Jack was not Jack at all. He was Mary. Or rather, she was Mary. And she was not twelve. She was sixteen. Her father was the late Jack Fenno and all the rest of her story was true enough, except her rude boot from Cornwall may have been prompted by the suspicion, unfounded as it turned out, that she had gotten herself in a family way without assistance from proper Church of England clergy. Or maybe it was with the assistance of a clergyman. Willie was a little vague on that part.

Regardless, she herself had hit on the idea of traveling as a boy. It offered greater hope for her physical safety and was a guarantee against future slurs on her reputation. Willie, of course, had known who she was from the instant we found her behind the potted plant in Virginia City.

His plan was to keep the charade in pantlegs long enough to "'atch a nistegg" in the 'Taint, then he could move her to San Francisco or maybe St. Louis where she could be educated properly and become a lady with nobody the wiser. To this end, the just and rightful execution of Joe Beans at the hands of Jimmy Adams was a useful adjunct.

Willie simply had not taken the roulette wheel's double-zeros into account. Mary had fallen in love with Jimmy.

"She's really in love with me?" Jimmy interrupted.

"Ya dense dolt. Where ya been fer the last three days?" Willie snapped.

The entire agenda was now floating in gumbo because Joe was still alive, and probably more than a little peeved, and someone may have noticed Mary's hand-tipping display of emotion on the dueling ground and suspect that something was seriously amiss in the Penrose/Fenno household.

During Willie's entire tirade, Jack (for I can not help thinking of her as anything except "Jack") sat on Willie's cot with eyes downcast and looked very much like a shop clerk caught with her hand in the cash drawer. Jimmy sat on the other side of the shack with the glazed demeanor of the second place finisher in a forty-round, bare-knuckle prizefight.

I thought Willie had given a tightly reasoned summary of the situation. He was a little skimpy on the prognostication possibilities, and he completely neglected mention of the omnipotent Major Crombernobie, but all and all his review would do justice to any five-act opus offered by Piper's Opera House.

As much as I wanted to throw roses at the feet of the cast and generally sing their praises for performances well done, I sat instead with muted yap and furrowed brow. For all I knew, Joe Beans was pouring kerosene 'round the cabin even as Willie spoke, or the Major was picking out blindfolds for our send-off party. We four seemed on more precarious ground than even Willie had allowed. My morbid foreboding was not relieved when Jimmy took the floor.

"Say what you will," his little speech began. "Much has happened and I can't understand it all. I only know one thing for sure. I haven't yet done what I came here to do."

"Ooooo, me little musketeer, do ya plan ta ask Joe Beans ta come ridin' down the middle o' the road agin in good light so ya ken fire off seven more rounds that go 'igh an' wide?" Willie asked. "Nay, me lad. Ya took 'im more or less by ambush taday, en 'is actions puzzle me. After ya spent yer bullets, why din't 'e come back an' take ya? 'E may be a bully an' by the looks o' it 'e may be a coward, but the man ken count. I ken't make sense o' it, but I'm certain 'e'll be ready fer ya now. I think ya should lie yerself low fer a spell."

"I'm sorry I missed him," said Jimmy. "But I'm not going to hide from him."

"Ken I say somethin'?" Jack interjected.

"Nay!" Willie barked at the girl. Then to Jimmy he said, "I was foolish ta let ya walk up ta 'im the way ya did taday an' ya won't do it agin. I 'ave nay wish ta see ya dead!"

"I can take him," insisted Jimmy. "I won't miss again."

Jack slapped her hand on Willie's cot and spoke louder than I'd ever heard her before, "I'm goin' ta speak me piece!"

"Be still, girl!" said Willie.

"Nay!" Jack shouted and stood up from the cot. "I've done everythin' ya've asked me, Uncle. An' I thank ya fer takin' me in. But I stand with Jimmy. If me own father 'ad been murdered I'd do the same an' so would you. More than ya men I nay wish ta see me Jimmy dead, but if 'e must die tanight then I ken only be by 'is side ta die with 'im."

"Oh good Jayzus an' Mary!" Willie cried.

Jack walked across the room and laid a hand on Jimmy's arm. "I love ya, James Buchanan Adams. If yer ta be walkin' into the night ta face this Joe Beans, then I'll be walkin' with ya."

Jimmy, who could look any man in the eye, stared straight at the floor when he muttered, "No, Mary. It'll be too dangerous for you."

"Yes!" she said. "We'll do the deed. An' we'll do it together." She picked up Jimmy's Winchester from the floor and handed it to him. "I love ya, Jimmy. Let's be done with it."

In disbelief of the scene, Willie put his head in his hands and repeated, "Jayzus an' Mary, Jayzus an' Mary."

Jimmy took the gun, considered the resolve of the young woman standing next to him, and then rose from his chair. "Let's go," he said. To Willie and me, he said, "You can come with us or stay, as you will."

In all honesty, a proposal to fry up some pork chops and wash them down with a few beers would have been a lot more to my liking. The idea of calling upon Joe Beans at this late hour was not high on my list of evening frivolities with polite society. But Willie seemed to have surrendered to the youngsters' impetuousness, so when he wordlessly stood and put on his coat, I tagged along in the name of family solidarity.

Looking for a man in Virginia City is one thing, requiring (as you have seen) stealth, patience, and a burro-load capacity for rye and water. Looking for a man in Bodie is a much simpler affair. There are only a half dozen saloons, and everybody in camp pretty much knows the cahoots of their neighbors. A manhunt in Virginia City could be a heavy chore for that old fellow Sisyphus, who labored all week long and Sunday, too. The same assignment in Bodie is a logroll, or leastwise it should be.

Willie, Jimmy, Jack and I poked into all six suds stops and caught not a whiff of Joe Beans. I was neither shocked nor surprised because the villain was probably lurking in the next alley and busy selecting arsenal and sharpening teeth. What did surprise me was that none of the boys had seen hide or hoof of Joe since he had vamoosed up Potato Peak. The collected wisdom of the crowd amounted to the conclusion that Joe had kept on riding straight through to Aurora and out of sheer humiliation he would never come back.

Willie and I impressed upon Jimmy and Jack that most miners are notorious for their shot-glass optimism. At night they could imagine a future of drinking champagne from ladies' slippers, but come the dawn, miners will still be washing their shirts in a chamber pot. So the boys' deduction about Joe's departure was no reason to drop our vigilance or muzzle our canon. A diamondback doesn't turn into a prairie dog just because you don't hear it rattle.

I will grant the men this much, our little avenging band of four had traipsed though Bodie as plain as ten-inch bull's eyes and had nary a puncture from pike or potshot to show for it. Undiscouraged by this pacificity, Jimmy decided to seek the bear in its den and convinced Willie to guide us toward Joe's domicile.

Jimmy was ready to march to the border of Hades and then wade across the river. Isn't it strange, but no matter how eager a man is to get himself killed, the love of a good woman always seem to spur him a bit faster to his destination.

We did not have to hike to Hades. We did not even have to walk as far as Joe's shack, because Joe was not there, and it was Jack who figured it out. "Wherever the man be," she lectured us, "I bet 'e'd be with that 'orse."

"Aye," said Willie. "They've always bin the heat an' smoke from the same fire. An' what benefit is that ta us, girl?"

"Where's he stable the 'orse?" she asked.

I immediately saw the solid logic behind the girl's argument and to advance her case I contributed that a missing object is always in the last place you look for it.

Yes, Willie allowed, a missing object is always in the last place you look for it, but that is only because after you find something, you would be a fine fool if you kept on looking for it.

While I mentally tested the validity of Willie's thesis, he conceded that the stable was a damned good place to investigate and we re-charted our course in its direction.

As the prime instrument of the 'Taint's discipline upon its laborers, Joe had access to the mine's private stable where all of management's beasts could slumber undisturbed by the horses and mules of us common folk. As soon as we could draw a bead on the structure we saw that a faint light was burning from within.

"If ya see 'im 'fore 'e sees us, this time jist take yer steady aim and shoot 'im. Ya won't be gettin' any second shots," Willie advised Jimmy. Then he signaled us to bend ourselves low, and thus contorted we skulked toward the barn.

Other than the soft crunch of our steps on the gravel, the night was as quiet as a tombstone. My heart was beating a lively fandango into my vest and I was praying that my cough wouldn't choose this occasion to start banging the lungs. Perhaps my pace was a trifle more cautious than the rest of the skulkers because Jack grasped my hand and towed me up to speed.

The double swinging doors of the barn were about six inches ajar, hence the emitted light. Jimmy slowly nosed his clear blue eyes into the opening and peered within. He pulled back and whispered, "I don't see him, but I'm going in."

"Git on yer belly," said Willie.

Jimmy nodded agreement, snaked close to the doors and carefully used his rifle barrel to widen the opening. The door screamed a creaky protest and my attempted retreat was only halted by Jack's tightened grip on my hand. For a goodly time we remained in icy tableaux. No blasts of mortar shell or Gatling gun cracked our frieze.

Jimmy turned to General Willie who pointed his consent to advance. The brave scout wormed his way through the doors and we could see nothing but his boots on the ground while we endured another lengthy pause. After a few lifetimes had passed, the boots disappeared and were followed quickly by Willie, and then by Jack, who dragged my pulsing vest into the ominously silent battle theater. Still, no gunshots or even saber rattles broke the calm.

Once inside the stable's walls we could see the source of the light. In front of a stall in the stable's deepest recess a lonely lantern hung from a post. Below the lantern was the monstrous profile of the unmistakable Old Scratch, and in the shadows cast by beasts and beams lurked all the rest of Satan's minions.

Jimmy got to his feet and stepped forward. Willie snatched hold of Jimmy's duster but the lad swiped the hand away and as if treading through quicksand he neared himself to the stall of Scratch. Jack and Willie and I remained near the entrance and snug to the mule-reeked earth.

It took a hunk of eternity, but Jimmy eventually reached the light. At the mouth of the stall he paused, peeked beyond the last foul partition, then lifted the Winchester's sight up to his eye into firing position. He stood straight up and aimed the rifle into the stall. I awaited a revengeful explosion.

Instead, there was only more silence.

Jimmy relaxed his stance, lowered the barrel, and softly waved us forward. Ha! I thought. The devil's not home tonight. But I was wrong.

When we reached Jimmy's side and looked into the stall for ourselves, we saw he was there. Piled into the corner behind his horse like a dung dump was Joe Beans, his bloodshot eyes looking straight into our own, and an empty whiskey bottle propped between his legs.

"I been waitin' for you, boy," Joe rasped.

"You know why I'm here," declared Jimmy.

"Yes. And I'm ready for you, I guess."

Joe picked up his bottle and studied the void in its bottom. Satisfied that no more comfort would be forthcoming, he looked to his left and right until he found the cork, then with overly meticulous care he pressed it into the bottle's mouth.

"I'm ready. Yes, I'm ... prepared," he slurred. "Two ... two things I'm gonna ask. Please."

"Yes?" said Jimmy.

"Make it with one shot. One shot ... right here." And with that, Joe poked himself approximately between his eyes. "Right here," he emphasized.

"Done," Jimmy answered. "What else?"

"Tell me ... tell me who told you."

"Spuds Halligan."

"Ah. Spuds. Sure. And ... and what did Spuds tell you?"

"You killed my father. Do you deny it?"

"Oh, no, I don't deny it. I killed your father. Andrew Jackson Adams! I killed him."

With that, Jimmy raised the rifle and the final moment of the Reckoning Day for Joseph Beans had apparently arrived. However, drunks don't always know when to shut up and stumble off stage. To this, Joe was no exception. He kept on talking.

"Andrew Jackson Adams ... a miserable coward who couldn't support his dear Susanna Shea ... who couldn't face her with his shame. I killed him. I left his little boy ... I left you, boy ... James Buchanan Adams ... I left you without a father."

"And now you'll pay for it!" Jimmy said.

"I killed him in Halligan's Saloon. I couldn't look at you or your mother another day ... so I killed him. I said, Andrew ... you're dead. Go away. And I did it. I went away. Shoot me, son. I'm the worst father that ever was. Your father deserves to die ... you deserve to kill him."

"You're a drunken madman!" Jimmy cried.

"Yes. I am that. And you are James Buchanan Adams, born to Susanna Shea Adams and Andrew Jackson Adams on January 31, 1860. And I am a drunken madman. Yes! I am Andy Adams, drunken madman. I killed off Andy Adams once a long time ago ... and I deserve to die again ... by the hand of my son, my one and only son. I am your father, Jimmy! Please! One bullet, son. One bullet ... right here!"

Jimmy lowered his gun and staggered backward two steps. His lips quivered and tears welled in his eyes. The brave scout who crept into this hellish barn looked now like a trembling orphan at a wake with strangers. He was struggling with demons none of us could have predicted. The ball had rolled into the double-zeros for Jimmy and no one except his father could advise him.

"Between the eyes!" Joe screamed. "Do it, son! Have the courage I never had."

Joe leaned back against the stall boards and closed the demanded targets.

Jimmy once again raised the rifle in earnest. Jack's breath sucked in and she near squeezed my hand to dust. Willie turned his back. As much as he loathed Joe Beans, he could not watch a son kill his own father. Every muscle in my body froze. It was the same empty feeling of inevitable dread that flashes through your gut the instant before a cave-in.

Bam! The Winchester reported.

Bam!

Bam!

Bam!

Bam!

Bam!

Bam!

The anger and hurt and frustration of a lifetime spent themselves through the seven bullets of Jimmy's Winchester repeating rifle.

The first bullet had gone right between Old Scratch's eyes and the horse had dropped without a neigh. Every subsequent slug had pounded into the animal's head and its blood and brains had splattered on the terrified and pitiful man huddled behind it.

When the firing stopped, the stable was shrouded in smoke and the sulfur stench of gunpowder. This, I thought, is what we unredeemed sluggards can look forward to after the final call.

Joe crawled over Scratch's carcass and hugged the horse's thick neck, smearing more blood between them until it was almost impossible to say who had taken the shots. He wept miserably as he lamented, "No, no, no ... not Old Scratch. Not you my friend. Not you. Not you."

Tears and sweat blackened by the smoke were dripping from Jimmy's chin. The rifle he dropped to the ground. He reached out his hand for Jack and said, "Let's go now. My business is done."

Nobody said another word. Nobody had to. We walked away.

The next morning I went over to Willie's cabin not knowing what I might advise them, but thinking they might welcome someone to fry the bacon and brew the coffee. Neither Willie nor Jack nor Jimmy was there and except for the sparse furniture, the place was cleaned out.

Willie had left me a letter on the table.

> Dear Friend,
>
> I think it wisest that I say goodbye to Bodie.
> I bought three horses from some of the night
> boys. Mary and Jimmy and me are heading for
> someplace else. I am sorry but I cannot tell you
> where. I am going to do right by these orphans so
> their lives can be better than our own.
>
> God bless you,
> William Penrose

It was not too much later in the day that Major Crombernobie caught up with me when I reported for timber trimming. I held no hopes for a bonus of any kind, and the Major did not exactly give me one. He proceeded to tick down my accomplishments to date:

I had not delivered Cousin Jack.

I had not delivered Willie Penrose.

In addition, the best mine bull in the history of the 'Taint had disappeared, and all the miners insisted that Joe Beans would never return.

To top it all off, there was a dead horse pumped full of lead in the company's stable.

The Major seemed to be of the mind that my contributions were not in the best interests of the officers or stockholders of the 'Taint Quite Borrasca Mine.

So he fired me.

I never again ran across Joe Beans or Willie or the two orphans. Although, years later I heard about a fellow named James Adams with a wife named Mary who made a great fortune in the goldfields of North Dakota, and I always wondered if maybe, just maybe, they were Jimmy and Jack.

As for me, I headed over to Aurora where I got a job in the Esmeralda Mines. I was back doing deep digging again. And it did not do my cough any good at all.

* * *

# The Independence Day Ball, 1872

In mid-spring of 1872, Kalamazoo and I went to the White Pine area where a camp called Treasure City was struggling along from the output of the Whudteweeno Mine. Treasure City had a well-deserved reputation for patriotic pride and community involvement. Only the year before, the citizens of this enlightened burg had lynched their mayor for succumbing to bribe taking. Other camps viewed this as an idealistic demonstration of participatory democracy which, if actually put into common practice, would result in a serious shortage of mayors.

Kalamazoo, however, was an ardent student of politics, having once run for alderman in Akron, Ohio, so he was eager to ingratiate himself to the local machine. It turned out to be an auspicious time for anyone looking to throw a hat into Treasure City's political ring.

We were in town but a day when I was struck with the clock-like organization and logic of the place. There were four saloons in town: the Silver Spoon, Jackson's, the Bonanza, and the Lucky Strike. By divine plan or just dumb coincidence, there were also four political parties. These mobs were the Happy Republicans (who drank at the Bonanza), the Unhappy Republicans (who took their poison at the Silver Spoon), the

Democrats (all of them unhappy and to be found at Jackson's), and the Great Rest of Us, who soaked it up pretty much anywhere we wanted but went to the Lucky Strike when we sought a little peace.

Not being well versed in these matters, I was surprised at the intricate structure of the set-up, and I marveled at its rich diversity. Kalamazoo assured me that all the great capitals in the Eastern states were run along similar lines, and that Treasure City was a paragon of partisan sophistication.

After we had fixed ourselves up with jobs at the Whudteweeno, we took to enjoying our evenings at the Lucky Strike. Kalamazoo had learned that this saloon, being neutral territory, would soon host a powwow where the muckymucks of all the City's tribes would sit down and chart the civic future of the place.

On the appointed night, One-Eyed Clyde, who owned the Lucky Strike, cleared the biggest table in the center of the place and the Great Rest of Us gathered around to bask in the historical import of the caucus. In came the stalwarts of the Happy Republicans led by Charlie the Chisel, a soft lard of a man who was the payroll clerk at the Whudteweeno. Next came the Unhappy Republicans whose boss was Billy Brown, a pinched-looking little fellow with spectacles, who owned the general store.

I was anticipating that the meeting would smack of the brouhaha flavor, but the boys all seemed amiable and soon set to drinking and speculating about where the Democrats were. After about an hour of this, Clyde dispatched the always-dependable Meatball Fred over to Jackson's to roust the rascals up.

Fred returned in less than ten minutes and told us that the Dems thought the meeting had been scheduled for next Friday. They were presently witnessing a heavily wagered cockfight, but they would be along as soon as it was over. The Republicans all muttered that such inconsideration was typical of Democrats. They ordered another round of drinks and set to arguing the merits of Jersey cocks as opposed to the more common Chinese cocks.

Eventually the Democrats completed the quorum when they staggered in behind their honcho, Irish Fitz. Irish was a big man. On the scales he would balance out with a mature jackass, although it is not likely anyone would voice that observation in his presence. He had fresh bloodstains over the front of his shirt, presumably from the cockfight, and you could tell from the get-go that Irish was a savvy politico.

"Here's what we're gonna do," Irish announced before he'd even sat down. "We're gonna petition the Legislature in Carson to incorporate White Pine as a county, with Treasure City as the seat. Then we're gonna build ourselves a courthouse with a statue of a nekkid lady out front of it, and at the same time we'll build ourselves a schoolhouse and maybe a lib'ary. And finally we're gonna build us one of them op'ry houses like I seen at Virginia City so Adah Menken can come here and dance in her pink tights."

Having stated his party's platform in as fine of an oration as I had ever heard, Irish sat down with a broad smile on his mouth and the cheers of the Great Rest of Us ringing in his ears. The Dems' agenda seemed to offer a little something for most everybody regardless of interest or persuasion. Which just goes to show you how wrongheaded we hanger-ons can be, because we had yet to hear from the Happy or Unhappy Republicans.

Right off the mark the Republicans did not say much. They let the applause die out, then Charlie the Chisel stood up.

"Well," he said. "Can't be done."

He sat down and all the rest of the Happy Republicans took to nodding their heads up and down like they had just heard from Moses after his confab with the Burning Bush.

Then Billy Brown stood up and proceeded to itemize a few of the more asinine deficiencies of the Dems' plan from the elevated view of the Unhappy Republicans. First off, he reminded us that a schoolhouse would not do anybody much good because there were not any little scrappers in camp, and a lib'ary was bald foolishness because near ninety percent of the boys cannot read and of those who can, about half of them do it in some foreign language or other. As to the op'ry house, Treasure City only had forty-three dollars and sixteen cents in the treasury, and that would not build anything Adah Menken would shake a feather in, much less shake a leg with her pink tights. Billy put a big finish on the pitch by observing that White Pine already had been incorporated as a county some two years back with Hamilton as the seat, so a courthouse would be superfluous. But he conceded that the statue of a nekkid lady might be an idea worth pursuing at some future date if it could be funded by purely voluntary contributions. Then he sat down.

Irish then stood up and said, "Is that so?"

Then he sat down.

Then Billie stood up again and said, "Yep."

Then he sat down, again.

I could tell that this politicking business could put an awful strain on a man's legs and hindquarters with all the standing up and sitting down it involved.

It also creates a powerful thirst. A short recess commenced while the parties rested their limbs and rejuvenated their windpipes with the available refreshments.

During this hiatus, and it is a closed book to me how the decision was arrived at, the convention chiefs hit on the notion of having a Fourth of July gala celebration, capped by an Independence Day Ball.

"That's it then," Irish announced to the Great Rest of Us. "Let's get us up some committees."

The Democrats right off made themselves the Flag Committee. Irish Fitz declared himself committee chairman and all the other Dems got to be vice-chairmen.

This seemed to irk the Unhappy Republicans who must have been kicking themselves for not thinking of it first. As a consolation to their wounded principles, they gobbled up the Ball of the Evening Committee with Billy Brown to chair and the vice duties being distributed in the traditional fashion.

The Happy Republicans admitted they could man the Music Committee with Charlie as chairman and his cronies taking the vice honors.

Irish then stood up again and called for a volunteer to be chairman of the Work Committee. Kalamazoo stepped forward and got the job on the spot by acclamation. It goes to show you how fast a man could rise to power in those days.

The business at hand having been completed to the satisfaction of each and all, the conflux adjourned with the party leaders dispersing to their respective clubs to plot and strategize.

In the days following, the holes in my knowledge about politics were stitched-in, courtesy of comrade Kalamazoo. For instance, Treasure City was not the only nest of Unhappy Republicans. My, no. They were all over the country.

You might remember that General Ulysses S. Grant was President of these United States at the time, and the Happy Republicans thought he was a good enough man who truly needed the work. They intended to re-elect him. But one day, according to Kalamazoo, some other Republicans decided they did not like the General anymore because he smoked cigars and drank whiskey, and maybe now and again let some of his boys slip off the job a tad before the shift whistle blew. So these Unhappy Republicans went off to Cincinnati and nominated their own man for President, a Mr. Horace Greeley, who ran a newspaper in New York City.

This was a grievous mistake in Kalamazoo's judgment. "Too much brains and not enough bourbon is their problem," he said.

The Happy Republicans paid no attention to the Unhappy ones. They pitched tent in Philadelphia and nominated the General amidst much patriotic fervor and unbridled carousing.

The Democrats had a convention too, although nobody knows why they bothered. They went to Baltimore, and with a curious absence of any imagination they nominated the same Mr. Horace Greeley favored by the Unhappy Republicans. All of the Democrats said they were against it, but they done it.

Politics is a strange and wondrous thing.

So during the month of June while the gangs in Treasure City were getting ready for their big July Fourth blowout, they (and I guess just about everybody else in the whole country) were getting het-up about this Grant or Greeley proposition.

As Chairman of the Work Committee, Kalamazoo had a ringside seat to all the backstage merriment. The Democrats summoned him over to Jackson's Saloon and they filled his head to the hairline with their scheme to make Ol' Glory the star attraction of the pageant. Irish had once passed through Cleveland on July Four and had seen how those Buckeyes hung flags from all the shops and hotels, and red, white, and blue bunting from the gaslight poles.

Kalamazoo assured Irish that Akron also embraced the custom, so he was familiar with the heavy-handed approach. Of course, Treasure City did not have as many buildings as Akron, nor was it yet graced with a single gaslight pole, but the heart of the plan was sound. We had a drink or two in honor of the patriotism of the great and sovereign state of Ohio, then had a drink or two over the vision of Treasure City fluttering awash a sea of Stars and Stripes.

The Flag Committee seemed satisfied that they had struck a pure vein and commissioned the Work Committee to smelt it up with all due speed.

Meanwhile, the Happy Republicans of the Music Committee were busy at the Bonanza Saloon concocting an inspiration for the appropriate philharmonics. After enticing Kalamazoo into their lair, they honored him by sharing what they had hatched. The plan had a nice symmetry to it, I will grant it that. The boys wanted two orchestras.

One should be a marching band, so a proper parade could spark the bash. Uniforms, they admitted, might be hard to come by. So, although highly desirable, were not absolutely necessary. But lots of fifes and drums and bugles were, as Charlie the Chisel emphasized, "dee reegor."

The second bunch should be a proper orchestra, with clean shirts, for the Ball of the Evening. This gang would be expected to serve up the waltzes in a big way, but also be able to rip out a few quadrilles because the Committee was anxious to cater to every musical taste.

The rye had flowed steadily during this conference and soon enough we were all contributing songs for inclusion in the orchestra's repertoire. Charlie was particularly helpful in this department, singing the ditties in a husky baritone voice with his vice-chairmen jumping in on the harmonies as best they could.

Before we got out of the Bonanza everybody had slapped Kalamazoo on the back and voiced abundant confidence that come the big day he would deliver the goods.

Over at the Silver Spoon, matters were not so much on the hunkydory note. The Unhappy Republicans in the Ball of the Evening Committee had detected a bothersome impediment to fulfilling their charter, and they drafted Kalamazoo to crack the thing.

A location for the soiree was not a problem. The Lucky Strike would fill the bill. It had the largest room in town and it even had a wood floor. So far, so good. The hitch, as Billy Brown pictured it, was that Treasure City had a rough population of three hundred and fifty men, and an exact population of two women. One of the gals was One-Eyed Clyde's wife, and the other was One-Eyed Clyde's wife's sister who was visiting from Elko.

This division of the sexes, which Billy ciphered as about a hundred and seventy-five to one, seemed somewhat light on the distaff participation. Could Kalamazoo offer a solution?

Kalamazoo allowed that it was a dicey question that on no account should be approached with a parched throat. The Unhappy Republicans quickly saw the sense in his words and ordered up generous portions of parch cleanser. Thus inspired, Kalamazoo assured the Committee that their worries were exaggerated and he would surely unknot the riddle in due course. For the rest of the night we applied the old throat oil but despite doubling and tripling the doses, the dawn came with us no nearer an answer than when we had begun.

As the last days of June scratched off the calendar I asked Kalamazoo how he aimed to clean his plate of the many political promises that he had so greedily heaped up. As near as I could tell, Fourth of July was a week away and he had not yet done anything but bend his elbow with the other big shots.

The Kal was not concerned.

"The secret to this politics racket," he told me, "is shovin' around the improbable until you got it pushed over to the impossible. Then you can pick up your pay and take the rest of the week off."

I did not see how this exactly applied to the situation, but Kalamazoo swore by it. The next day he commandeered an orchestra.

Well, calling it an orchestra is putting more weight into the word than the pure facts would normally bear. Kalamazoo called it an orchestra. Most anyone else in town would call it Henry Pike. That was his name, Henry Pike. Henry was a broken down old sourdough who could play the "Arkansas Traveller" on a fiddle.

Kalamazoo pointed out that not only was Henry the only man within a hundred miles who could play a musical instrument. Henry was also the only man who owned one. Then too, it would save the Music Committee a big hunk of their budget by having the marching band double up as the dance orchestra. All Henry would have to do is change his shirt.

Anyone who complained that Henry only knew the one song was just not examining the thing from the proper perspective. As long as we assigned somebody to limit Henry's whiskey intake to no more than three drinks an hour, there was no reason that the geezer could not play "Arkansas Traveller" all night long.

I will admit that fiddle music is not my own favorite. Most diggers when given a choice of hearing fiddle music or a polecat being buggered by a black bear, would vote for the latter. Not that there is usually much difference. But Henry Pike's fiddle playing, provided you were partial to the "Arkansas Traveller," was not too disagreeable.

The plan to shower the town with flags and bunting proved considerably more challenging. Kalamazoo learned that the nearest flag was probably in Austin, one hundred and twenty miles away, a three-day journey each way. Even if somebody was willing to make the trip and filch the flag from Austin, they still could not make it back in time.

This stumped Kalamazoo for quite awhile. He looked at the problem one way. Then he looked at it from the other direction for a spell. No matter from what point of the compass he approached it, it was bafflement. He spent the best part of an entire Sunday starring into his whiskey until at last he slapped his hand on the table and shouted, "We'll just have to patch one together for ourselves."

Off he marched to Billy Brown's store with me in tow. Kalamazoo explained the difficulty to Billy, but satisfaction was not the first item returned across the counter. Any chance of requisitioning the proper materials seemed stymied by two aspects of the deal.

Firstly, the milk of human kindness seemed a shade low in Billy's personal inventory. As a dedicated Unhappy Republican he insisted that Democrats were lazy skunks who were lollygagging all around the country when Uncle Horace needed their help, and wasn't it just like them to wait until the last minute before getting something as simple as a flag. Secondly, he didn't stock any red or blue fabric of any variety and the only white cloth he had was some tent canvas, and the Democrats would sure as hell get charged for anything they used.

This might have defeated a lesser man than Kalamazoo. He must have had a little Minuteman blood in him because quick as a matchstick he snatched up the tent canvas and assured Billy that the Democrats would pay top dollar. We were out the door before Billy could introduce any where-fors or where-ases on the negotiations.

Encouraged by his progress to date, Kalamazoo made the rounds of the four watering holes and polled the denizens about items red and items blue. No one confessed to owning such luxuries. The always-dependable Meatball Fred at the Lucky Strike, however, swore that when he helped move Charlie the Chisel into his digs, Fred had seen a calico quilt with a red lining. For no extra charge Fred threw in the scoop that Charlie was off deer hunting until next Tuesday, but if Kalamazoo was so eager to lay his hands on some quilts maybe he should try that Mormon fellow who set up camp yesterday over in the gulch near Hamilton Hill.

This intelligence seemed to brighten Kalamazoo considerably. He ran out of the Strike and kicked his heels in the air. I could not see how we were any better off than we had been before.

"Don't you see it? We're halfway home!" he said. "A Mormon fellow. Why, I bet the poor sot must have at least ten or twelve wives. What with all of them running around and clogging up the outhouse and such, he's sure to let us borrow a few of them for the ball."

I had to admit that the prospect showed promise.

Kalamazoo instructed me to obtain a jug of cheap stuff and meet him at our cabin in half an hour, as he had one more appointment before we could address this Mormon development. I did as told, and Kalamazoo showed up as promised. Under his arm he carried a large calico quilt with a lining redder than an Arizona sunset. He was pleased to report that Meatball Fred had been accurate in the Charlie the Chisel portion of his testimony and now we could venture to the gulch near Hamilton Hill to verify the Mormon aspect.

We took grasp of the jug and proceeded to walk the four miles out to the gulch. All along the way he hammered in the point that Charlie certainly would be gratified to learn that his quilt would be a part of Treasure City's historic Independence Day celebration. Charlie's untimely absence might have caused him otherwise to forfeit the honor, but Kalamazoo's prompt and decisive action had once again saved the bacon.

"The whole Seventh Cavalry of the United States Army," he modestly burped to me, "couldn't do much better."

At Hamilton Hill we wandered here and yon through the ravine for a time until we exhausted most of our spit and half of our jug. At last we stumbled on a campsite with the following contents: two creaky-looking covered wagons, two whip-scarred oxen, two underfed mules, one ancient specimen of a Mormon, and one equally aged and shriveled sample of a Mormon wife.

You may have noticed, as we did, the inventory lacked the desired plethora of young Mormon brides giggling modestly in the background. Nevertheless, we howdy-dewed the patriarch and after he set aside his shotgun, the three of us sat down for a neighborly visit.

His name was Ezekiel Peepers and we offered him the jug, but he declined it. Mormons, we were saddened to hear, abhor intoxicants in any form. For a teetotaler he was friendly enough. We begin chatting up the weather, and the trails, and the Indian troubles and other such small talk, and in no time at all you would have thought we were a lodge of Odd Fellows at the regular Saturday night hooha.

Eventually, Kalamazoo worked the conversation around to the wife census. Zeke was not embarrassed by the topic. It seems that we "Gentiles" as he called us, are always badgering the "Saints" with questions about the spouse count. Zeke confided to us, man to man, that he wasn't all that good of a Saint, and maybe he would have a taste or two from that jug after all, and he was a poverty-struck son of Job and every effort to the contrary had gone bust. He had but the one wife and it was a struggle to feed her and the mules and the oxen, too. So with it all he had never seriously considered adding another mate to the load. Why, he did not even have the wherewithal to put shoes on the feet of his four daughters.

Kalamazoo almost spit up his swallow, but contained himself enough to ask, "And might those dear girls be traveling with you?"

"Ruth!" Zeke called out. "Fetch up the girls."

I am at a loss to tell you where the young ladies had been stashed, but out they came, clearly proving that Zeke had not exaggerated their number. They were as barefooted as he had painted them and, although no beauties, they were not an unpleasant looking litter. The youngest appeared to be around twelve with the eldest about sixteen. One of them wore a blue gingham cloak, and Kalamazoo said later that it made her the prettiest in his eyes by far.

Zeke's introductions had the terse cordiality much favored by the rare Nevada family man. "This is Esther. This is Micah. This is Obadiah. And this is Lamentations. Now you girls, git!"

As the girls dutifully returned to hiding, Zeke explained for our Gentile benefit, "I named 'em after my favorite Hebrew Bible books."

"And fine, healthy girls they are!" Kalamazoo chimed. "Maybe in the spirit of Christian brotherhood, there's some way us citizens of Treasure City can help you out."

It was after sundown before Kalamazoo and I returned to our shack. For all his poverty, Zeke was no green horse trader, and Kalamazoo was a shrewd broker himself. They had haggled up one broach and bargained down another. They had offered and counter offered and squirmed and squealed until finally the deal was all cooked up.

The contract, as shaked upon, called for the party of the first part (Ezekiel Peepers) to provide four daughters and one wife at the Independence Day Ball for purposes of chaste and respectable dancing only. The party of the second part (the good citizens of Treasure City as represented by Kalamazoo) would provide the party of the first part with the sum of twenty-three U. S. American dollars and five pairs of shoes, a pair for each daughter and wife Ruth.

As a token of good faith, the parties exchanged some gewgaws on the spot. Kalamazoo got Obadiah's blue gingham cloak, and Zeke got four bits plus what remained in the jug.

Kalamazoo believed he had gotten the best of the whole deal.

"I was going to throw in the shoes anyways because the girls could never dance barefoot on that splintery floor at the Strike," he boasted.

I was not as sure. It seemed to me that the shoe amendment only begged the question of where the twenty-three U. S. American dollars were coming from, unless the good citizens of Treasure City were prepared to part with more than half of the burg's stockpile. I could not deny, though, that the blue cloak transaction seemed to favor the party of the second part.

With the jubilee scheduled for the coming Thursday, by Tuesday the town's patriotic kettle was a nearing a boil. Maybe in Akron, Ohio, they favored the Sunday school picnic approach to Independence Day, but here in Treasure City the temper looked more like a Tong war.

Billy Brown was beating the bushes for the Uncle Horace vote, and Irish Fitz was boosting the notion that the choice between Greeley and Grant was the same as choosing t'wixt strychnine and hemlock. Charlie the Chisel had returned from deer hunting and discovered that some scalawag had pinched his prized quilt. With an understandable justification he suspected that Irish Fitz was the culprit, and Charlie was not bashful to say so.

Kalamazoo's policy was to drink the straight party ticket. That is to say, in the Bonanza he toasted the General. In the Silver Spoon he hoisted in the name of the Honorable Horace. In Jackson's he cursed them both and imbibed on the philosophy that the whole damn country was going to hell in a dogcart.

During the intermissions Kal dug into putting the flourishes on Ol' Glory. He laid out the white tent canvas, and Charlie's red calico quilt, and Obadiah's blue gingham cloak on our cabin's dirt floor. With his jackknife and a set of wire clips borrowed from the Whudteweeno, he carefully cut the materials into the properly sized stripes and field. Nailing down the correct star count was nettlesome. After more than a few hours of stimulating thought and conversation, we decided that the Union had thirty-seven states, provided Colorado had not snuck in when nobody was paying attention.

We were ignorant of the latest official configuration of stars on the field, but figured alternating rows of seven and eight was probably as close as anybody would get. We sewed it up using twine and a tent awl, and I will say that Betsy Ross herself could not have done much better under the circumstances.

On the eve of the Fourth, Kalamazoo scoured the metropolis for shoe contributions. He knew that simply passing the collection basket was unlikely to conjure up the soles, so he based his solicitation campaign on two inarguable facts. Most of the boys had, in addition to their work boots, a pair of half boots or brogans tucked away in their gripsacks. And a goodly number of the boys, especially on the night before a holiday, would be passed out drunk in their bunks by midnight. Fact number one plus fact number two added up to five pairs of handsome shoes before morning, with Kalamazoo taking special care to choose donors of the small-footed species.

Showing me the booty, Kalamazoo was rightly proud. "Each and every one contributed without complaint," he said.

The dawn's early light on July Four brought the kind of gleaming golden day that makes a man want to whistle "Yankee Doodle" on his way to the morning latrine. The birds were atwitter, the sky was cloudless blue, the sun was as agreeable and gentle as a mother's kiss, and all the saloons were opened early to accommodate the celebrating throngs. There was a happy and excited stir of anticipation in the crowd, the likes of which I had not seen since Arthur Perkins Heffernan was hanged by the neck in Virginia City.

Just like at the Heffernan hanging, Treasure City's little beanfest started fashionably late. The parade was supposed to originate in front of Jackson's at noon, but because The Great Rest of Us had been in the saloons since nine o'clock, it took about an hour for the committee vice-chairmen to put the prod on the boys.

With that task completed, the principals gathered in the street to await the starter's pistol. Irish Fitz and the Democrats were beaming from Jackson's porch. They had affixed the flag to a tent pole and were waving it over their heads as if ready to re-enact the second Battle of Bull Run. Being the Flag Committee, they would have the honor of leading the procession which, if the playbill was accurate, was plotted to march past the other saloons before arriving at the Lucky Strike where the Literary Exercises would commence in front of the horsewater trough. "Literary Exercises" was how they were billing the speeches.

Billy Brown and the Unhappy Republicans were present, and they appeared patriotically happified by the attendance of Esther, Micah, Obadiah, and Lamentations. Kalamazoo and I were likely the only celebrants who noticed Ezekiel Peepers hovering around the girls like a momma bear with cubs. One-Eyed Clyde's wife and her sister were also present and accounted for, and with Ruth that made seven women! So the Ball of the Evening Committee was already congratulating itself for assuring the success of the shindig. Of course Kalamazoo was there, busy fitting the girls and ma Peepers with their new shoes and giving Zeke the snake-oil treatment about the twenty-three U. S. American dollars.

Charlie the Chisel and the Happy Republicans were in the street and working the crowd into the proper mood by singing "The Battle Hymn of the Republic," and "Oh, Susanna."

The dramatis personae were complete when Henry Pike and his fiddle were hauled onto the scene by Henry's appointed bodyguard, the always-dependable Meatball Fred.

When Henry started in on "Arkansas Traveller," Irish Fitz clamped himself to the tent pole and led the jolly herd up the boulevard toward the Bonanza. It is a credit to the populace that we did not lose too many of the boys there while Charlie and company gave a reprise of "Mine eyes have seen the glory … " to those who had missed the first showing. Nor did our numbers significantly dwindle at the Silver Spoon, so the troops arrived at the Lucky Strike with ranks intact and colors flying.

The curtain rose on the Literary Exercises with Billy Brown stepping up on the horsewater trough and from this podium he addressed the masses on the topic of "Our Founding Fathers."

He started in about Christopher Columbus tripping over America on his way to someplace else, then he glad-handed the Pilgrims for sticking fish in the ground and thinking up Thanksgiving, and he started piling it on about those brave lads who dumped tea into Boston Harbor, which led him to what a no-good tyrant King George was. If Billy had stopped right then, the gallery would have given him hearty applause and maybe would have asked him to take a bow. But something about King George's villainy reminded Billy about General Grant and he began to color his remarks accordingly.

"The cheatin', lyin', taxin' termite of a King tried to strangle the life out of American freedom just like that president in Washington is trying to do today!" He told us.

Then he went on to pump up Ben Franklin and Tom Jefferson and all the boys who signed the Declaration of Independence and cracked the Liberty Bell. More and more his comments were leaning to the King George and General Grant comparison and pretty soon he got to George Washington whom he favorably likened to Horace Greeley.

This was too much for Charlie the Chisel. He yelled out, "Slander! Scandalous slander! You're a horse's ass, Billy Brown!"

There is nothing like a heckler to get the audience's attention and we all pressed in a little tighter so as not to miss any of the asides.

"You'll get your chance, Charlie." Billy countered. "It's just like the Grant boys to stifle free speech. They've stolen everything else in Washington so now they're out to trample on the Bill of Rights."

"Horsefeathers!" yelled Charlie.

But Billy ignored him and resumed the glorious tale of how George Washington nearly froze his bunions off at Valley Forge but finally managed to save the country, just like Horace Greeley would do if elected.

When Billy stepped down from the trough the Unhappy Republicans gave him a brain-rattling cheer and the Democrats joined the Happy Republicans in blowing the raspberries and generally demonstrating their foulest disapproval. The Great Rest of Us set our hands to clapping. Not so much because we endorsed Greeley or opposed Grant, but more because we appreciated a lively show.

The Peepers clan watched the proceedings in silent wide-eyed amazement. Being Mormons, maybe this was their first taste of American politics and they did not know what to make of it. Kalamazoo, meantime, was avoiding Zeke by helping One-Eyed Clyde pack full whiskey bottles out of the Strike and haul the empty ones back in.

Charlie stepped up on the trough next, and now it was the turn of the Happy Republicans to beat their drums while the Democrats and Unhappy Republicans played the hissing role. The title of Charlie's oration had been announced as "The Union: Now and Forever," and he wasted no time in getting on with it.

"A half score and one year ago, this nation was torn asunder by a pack of traitorous rebels," he began. "And now another pack of disloyal coyotes are joining the Democrats and trying to do it again!"

As an opening it was a real lollapalooza and stirred the listeners to loudly voice their opinions pro and con. Irish Fitz shook his fist and screamed, "Grant is robbing us blind!"

"The General saved us from your kind once, and God willing he'll do it again!" Charlie barked. And speaking right over the hoots and guffaws, he told us that President Grant had assumed the mantle of Abraham Lincoln while small-minded hypocrites of the other parties were flimflamming the public with a New York City charlatan who could best be compared to Jefferson Davis on a bad day.

Charlie blathered on for close to an hour with an admirable selection of variations on his chosen theme, while the Dems and the Unhappies were getting more vocal in their opposition, and One-Eyed Clyde and Kalamazoo were quickening their pace in and out of the Lucky Strike. By the time Charlie concluded his oration with a call to return "the Messiah of the Republic" to four more glorious years in the White House, the hordes were indiscriminately howling their enthusiasm or agitation without prompting from the speaker.

The heat and the dust, and the concentration necessary to follow the gist of spoken arguments, can take a toll on men that requires strong restoration. Irish Fitz, as the next scheduled presenter, had hit the phlegm cutter with particular generosity. Irish stumbled onto the trough, using the flagpole for much needed support, and burst forth a speech supposedly entitled "E Pluribus Unum."

"Grant and Greeley are both rattleshnakes! If either one of 'ems shelected we all oughta move to Utah where they ain't got no gov'nment!" Irish had coined the most moving slogan of the afternoon, and move the rabble it did. The front-row ticketholders were almost pushed into the horsewater by the surge from the balcony contingent.

Even Ezekiel Peepers was deeply touched by Irish's words.

"It's a lie! It's a lie! Utah is the Promised Land!" he called out to no one in particular. "It is Zion! It is Zion!" he screamed, as if that would make a difference.

Billy Brown jumped up on the trough and grabbed two handfuls of Irish Fitz's lapels. "I want my money for the tent canvas and I want it now!" he demanded.

"What?" Irish said. "What're you shaying?" Turning to Charlie, who was angrily swinging his hat in the air, Irish asked, "Whatch he shaying?"

"He used my tent canvas in the flag and now he won't pay for it!" Billy yelled at Charlie.

Charlie looked closely at the flag and the issues hastily clarified themselves in his mind. "That's my quilt!" he gasped. To emphasize the point, he added, "That's my quilt!"

"I want my money!" demanded Billy.

"I want my quilt!" Charlie screamed.

"I want my twenty-three dollars!" Zeke threw in.

"What? What? What?" Irish kept repeating.

Releasing Irish, Billy firmly grasped the flag. "If you won't pay me, I'm takin' it!" he yelled at Irish.

"That's my quilt!" repeated Charlie.

"I want my twenty-three dollars!" Zeke thundered.

"What?" Irish loudly wondered.

Seeing the possibility of forever losing his beloved blanket, Charlie grasped the end of the flag not held by Billy. Irish had no intention of surrendering Ol' Glory and was in danger of losing his balance, so he clutched a heretofore unclaimed corner of the banner. A triangular tug-of-war began with none of the contestants able to claim the initial advantage.

Kalamazoo apparently felt the entertainment as staged was still inadequate. He loudly instructed Henry Pike to "Play something. Play something!"

Henry played the only something he knew, and now the tug-of-war on the horsewater trough was musically accompanied by the "Arkansas Traveller," with vocal interpretations provided by Zeke, who kept calling to the heavens for his twenty-three dollars, and over three hundred intoxicated miners who were screaming and laughing and pushing one another toward a grand frenzy.

The action in the center ring came to its logical conclusion when the portion of flag pulled by Billy, and the portion pulled by Charlie parted company with a screeching rip that sent Irish and his share of Ol' Glory into the horsewater.

Then Charlie pulled back his fist and punched Billy square in the left eyeball. This was the cue for all the Happy Republicans to poke their fists into the noses of the Unhappy Republicans who promptly retorted in kind.

Seeing that his demand for financial satisfaction was going unheeded, Ezekiel Peepers upheld the honor of his strange tribe by cracking Irish Fitz over the head with the broken remains of the flagstaff. The action spurred the Democrats to take revenge on the Great Rest of Us and, for reasons that may forever be lost in the haze of history, prompted Henry Pike to break his fiddle over the bean of the always-dependable Meatball Fred.

While the womenfolk took refuge in the relative safety of the Lucky Strike, we political initiates continued to brawl in the street until every last one of us was knocked unconscious or was too tired to get there. It took awhile, but the survivors eventually made their way back to their favorite haunts and nursed their wounds with more whiskey, and agreed pretty much to a man that this was the best damn Fourth of July celebration they had ever had.

Anyway, it got my vote.

In the event that you are ignorant of the national election results, I can tell you that General Grant thrashed Mr. Greeley something terrible and returned to the White House. Mr. Greeley was taken to an insane asylum where he died.

Kalamazoo did all right for himself. He got elected to the State Legislature and went to Carson City. Later he was elected to the United States House of Representatives and went to Washington, D. C. But that is the last that anybody from these parts ever heard of him.

\* \* \*

# The Hucksters' Mire

My comings and goings around Nevada cannot always be blamed on an inability to hold down a job. Sometimes I take my leave with an eye toward financial betterment. Sometimes a local citizenry adopts a moral stance above my own. And sometimes I move on for the unencumbered hell of it.

On some occasions my coming improves the average quality of a mine or camp; on other occasions my going has the same effect. Most times I simply arrive or depart with all the influence of a snowflake in spring.

Not all men are like me, of course. Some fellows just naturally upgrade the climate of a place. Others inevitably blacken the air. In Nevada this is particularly noticeable when you travel, and it is another reason I like to do it so much.

In May of 1880, I decided Carson City would offer more variety and enrichment than Aurora, so I booked passage on the Smith Valley Coach Line. On the appointed day I presented myself at Glasscock's Saloon, which served as the coach line's southern terminus. There I met my five fellow trip-takers while we awaited the hitching and loading of the coach.

As blind luck and my own peripatetic history would have it, I was acquainted with three of the passengers: Ephraim

Kupperkeeper, Solomon Gould, and the always-dependable Meatball Fred (whose last name escaped me then and escapes me to this day). The two new ones to me were Riley Grannan, a miner from Kentucky, and Walter Hollis, a carpenter who lived out Belmont way.

"Do you remember me?" I asked the always-dependable Meatball Fred.

Fred looked me over crown to toes, and then judged, "No, can't say as I do."

"Last I saw of you was in Treasure City when Henry Pike broke his fiddle over your head," I reminded him.

"I recall that well enough. I still got the bump," he said. "It's you that I can't place."

"Well, no matter," I assured him. Fred, as you can see, was not really always dependable. But he was still a good man.

Ephraim Kupperkeeper and Solomon Gould were a pair of hucksters who I had met on this same stage line when Willie Penrose brought his orphans to Bodie. Kupperkeeper sold hand tools and Gould sold tunnel track. I do not think they worked as a team. They just happen to be traveling together then, and they were traveling together now. The two of them were instructing the barkeep on how to mix some elaborate concoction called a Sacramento Sling, so I did not have an early chance to say how-do.

Instead, I made acquaintance with Riley Grannan and Walter Hollis. Walter was delivering some legal papers to Carson City for his father-in-law. Riley was going to Virginia City because he had never been there and he did not believe the stories about the place. Both these boys bought me a beer and listened to my advice about the pitfalls of big cities. They were good, honest men.

Our pleasant jawing and drinking halted when Eugene Blair, a master teamster, announced the rig was fit for sojourn. It is always a comfort to see your driver is a veteran and not some whip-mad young blue-blazer. Eugene had patience and experience carved into every crease of his wind-burned face.

"Drink 'em down boys," Eugene instructed. "And take a piss. Get yerselves aboard and we'll go."

Kupperkeeper and Gould were not yet satisfied with the barkeep's efforts on the Sacramento Sling and they remained salooned. Walter, Riley, Fred, and I followed the orders to the letter. When we four finished our natural duties out back and returned for boarding, the two hucksters were closely interrogating Eugene.

We heard Gould saying, "I was personally assured by John Mackay, who is a major stockholder in this line, that every precaution is being taken."

"That's right, sir. But precautions ain't no guarantee," Eugene told him. "If it's any comfort, more trips than not don't get stopped at all."

Kupperkeeper then jumped in. "If you and everybody in Lyon County knows it's Milton Sharp, I can't understand why you don't go out and arrest him."

Eugene sighed and explained, "That's the plan. It just ain't happened yet."

"The facility with which this 'Gentleman Bandit' operates suggests collusion in my mind," Gould said.

"Milton Sharp usually does the jobs alone. That's partly why he's been so hard to collar," said Eugene.

Gould sneered, "That's not what I'm getting at."

"Mister Gould, I am going to ignore any inference in that," said Eugene. "Ever since we added an apprentice driver with a shotgun, Sharp hasn't stopped us. We got Willis Knowles riding today. I can't see as how we can do much more."

Kupperkeeper was hardly satisfied. "Only an apprentice? Why don't you have a bonafide Pinkerton man? Or better yet, a Lyon County deputy?"

Eugene was not ruffled. He shrugged, "Since Willis has been on I ain't been held up once."

"Ben Holladay's line doesn't have this kind of trouble," Gould charged.

"Holladay's line has just as much trouble as anybody's. He just don't have Milton Sharp, that's all," replied Eugene.

"I loaned Old Ben the money to start up," said Kupperkeeper.

"You don't say," said Gould. "He and I get together every year in St. Joe for his birthday. I'll say hello for you."

"I can say howdy to Old Ben for myself just about anytime I've a mind to. Thank you just the same," Kupperkeeper said.

Gould said, "Don't take offense, Ephraim."

Kupperkeeper said, "I'm not taking anything. Especially from you, Solomon."

All the rest of us passengers passed by them as we piled into the coach. Eugene Blair followed us and he climbed into the driver's box next to Willis Knowles. Eugene shouted out, "All aboard that's coming aboard!"

Kupperkeeper and Gould emerged from Glasscock's casual as whiskers. They were apparently still debating the measure of their friendships with Ben Holladay.

"Git up!" Eugene yelled to the horses and cracked his whip.

"Whoa! I ain't on!" screamed Gould.

"A little courtesy please, Blair!" shouted Kupperkeeper.

Eugene reined in and the two malingerers loaded on. Upon entry they wiggled into the remaining spaces between Riley and me on one side and Fred and Walter on the other.

"What line of work are you gents in?" inquired Kupperkeeper.

We told him. Fred went to some detail in explaining he was a "general helper" who took anything that was offered, or that was not locked up in a strongbox. Gould and Kupperkeeper did not even chuckle.

"Any of you boys actually employed at present?" asked Gould.

No, we all confessed. Although we each had confidence our circumstances would improve before summer.

That did it for small talk until Kupperkeeper said, "Mr. Hollis, could I trouble you to change seats with me? I hate to admit it but I get sick if I have to ride backwards. One time I vomited going down Geiger Grade. Before you knew it, everybody else in the coach had churned up their guts too. Oh, it was an awful mess."

Walter said, "It's all the same to me." And he traded positions with Kupperkeeper.

This put Walter between Riley and me riding backwards, and Gould between Fred and Kupperkeeper riding forwards.

We clunked along wordlessly for a while until Gould broke into a violent coughing spell.

"I'll be all right," he rasped. "Don't worry about me. It'll pass." But he went on coughing like the Black Death had hold of him. I handed him my short bottle of rye. He partook liberally but the coughing only stopped when he was actually swallowing the poison. In between belts he was hacking like a pile driver.

"It's the alkali *(cough)*," he said. "The alkali blows in *(cough)* and it gets up my cough *(cough)*."

"Can you not do anything for it?" asked Riley.

"Not much," said Gould as he took another guzzle of my whiskey. "Well, maybe *(cough)* if my back was to it *(cough)*, it would help *(cough, cough)*."

"Is it over here you want to be sitting?" suggested Riley.

"Sure *(cough)*, it's worth a try."

So Riley and Gould swapped seats and now Kupperkeeper and Gould were facing each other on the driver's side of the coach. I don't know if credit was due to the new seating arrangements or to the last drop in my rye bottle, but Gould's cough cleared up and he was now able to engage Kupperkeeper in uninterrupted eyeball to eyeball conversation.

When I say "uninterrupted," I mean if their words were bricks they would make a building solid as a church. There was not a hint of air between man, word, paragraph, chapter, volume, or collected works. After six miles it reminded me of the time at the Colossus Mine when a drunk machinist put the blowing pumps in reverse. The oxygen started sucking right up through the vents and all the boys made a gagging charge for the exits. On a moving stagecoach, of course, you do not have any exits.

And such hornswoggle it was! These fellows, according to their own testimony, had grossed more money in the sale of hand tools and tunnel track than all the mines of the Comstock had produced in silver or gold. They had tipped off every lucky prospector about where to hit the pay dirt. They had advised every financier on when to buy or dump stock. They had bribed every senator in the Nevada legislature and had guzzled brandy with the governor. And every madam in every bordello from Bumm's Hole to San Francisco always provided them services on the house.

Fifteen or so miles out of Aurora, Gould finally gave it a pause. "I gotta piss," he proclaimed.

"So do I," said Kupperkeeper. He poked his head out and yelled, "Blair! Blair! Stop the coach!"

"What's wrong?" shouted Eugene.

"Stop the coach!" Kupperkeeper repeated.

Gould put his face out into the alkali and chimed, "You must stop!"

The coach came to a dusty halt.

We heard Eugene yell down to us, "What the hell's the matter?"

"Gotta pee," said Gould leaving the coach.

"Me too," said Kupperkeeper following him.

"Goddamnit!" cried Eugene. "If Milton Sharp is here'bouts, he'd sure enjoy us stopping for him."

"Then I suggest you watch out for him instead of watching us!" replied Gould.

"For God's sake, hurry it up!" said Eugene.

"You tend to your business," Kupperkeeper said. "And we'll tend to ours."

The rest of us passengers fidgeted in the coach and peered anxiously out the windows. The prospect of near-at-hand bandits tends to put honest men on edge.

Kupperkeeper and Gould relieved themselves in the sand and climbed back aboard.

"Carry on, Blair," commanded Gould.

"Thank you!" Eugene spit.

"He's a cheeky buster," Kupperkeeper observed.

Eugene got the team back up to speed and in the coach the air started getting thin again. After six more miles of non-stop blather, the almost always reliable Meatball Fred said, "Why don't you boys put a lid on it?"

Gould said, "Why don't you think about getting useful employment?"

"Maybe you could think about givin' us a rest," said Walter.

"Maybe you could think about kissing my arse!" said Kupperkeeper.

"Let's throw the both of 'em out on their fannies," suggested Riley.

"I'm for it," said Walter. "Can we get the driver to stop again?"

"Shit on that," said Fred. "We'll toss 'em on the move."

"You boys are flirting with thirty days in the hoosegow," said Gould.

"Thirty days?" said Kupperkeeper. "I'll get them all hung!"

"Either way, we'd be getting some peace," Riley offered.

It is not possible for the driver to hear conversation within a moving coach, no matter how vehement the discussion. So all of us were stunned into a shut-up when the vehicle rolled to a stop.

A loud warning came from Eugene, "Don't nobody get out!"

"Ohmygawd! It's Milton Sharp," said Gould.

"Where?" demanded Kupperkeeper.

"Why else would we be stopping?" countered Gould.

"We can hide our watches in our boots," said Kupperkeeper.

"Watch, hell. I'm hiding my money belt," said Gould.

"Oh, very easy for you. Only my money belt won't fit in my boot," said Kupperkeeper.

While the hucksters were stashing their valuables, Eugene appeared on the ground beside us. He held his shotgun. "Well," he said. "We got us a problem."

"Is it Sharp?" asked Gould.

"I don't honestly know," answered Eugene. "There's an oak layin' 'cross the road in the gorge up there. Might be Milton Sharp slowin' us up. Might not."

"Then let's move the damn thing and get going!" ordered Kupperkeeper.

"Don't look movable short of nightfall, if then," said Eugene.

"Let's go 'round it then," said Gould.

"Ain't room," stated Eugene.

Kupperkeeper stuck his chin out the window and said, "You're pretty sure about what you can't do, Blair. What *can* you do?"

"Well, right now I got Willis keeping a sharp eye out," said Eugene.

"Fine. That's fine," said Gould. "So are we going to sit here 'til the damn tree rots and we can just drive over it?"

Eugene took his time in answering. He looked up the road. Then he looked back in the coach. Then he looked up the road again. "Well, that's one plan, Mister Gould. Although that's not the one I'd recommend."

Walter asked, "What do ya want us to do, Mister Blair?"

"I guess that's up to you boys. We got three things we might go for. Four, if you count Mister Gould's suggestion. We could take the time to try and move the oak. We'd probably have to unhitch the team and drag it. You fellas would have to do the work because Willis and I would be on lookout."

"John MacKay is going to hear about this," commented Kupperkeeper.

"Another thing's we could turn back to Aurora and wait for a crew to get here and clear the way."

"That could take two days," said Gould.

"Probably more," corrected Eugene. "Or, we could take a chance on the Yellow Creek Mine Road. It starts about a mile back and dumps in again 'bout three miles up. Thing about that is the Yellow Creek Mine ain't been operating for a while, so I can't speak for the condition of the trail. It's up to you boys. Don't make much difference to Willis and me."

"I'm not keen on the idea of returning to Aurora," said Kupperkeeper.

"There's too much alkali about for me to consider any tree removals," said Gould.

"Then we agree, we'll take the detour," said Kupperkeeper.

"That's how I see it," said Gould.

"That's two votes," said Eugene. "Are the rest of you boys for it?"

Because Eugene's offered choices all seemed to promise more time in the company of Kupperkeeper and Gould, I don't think any of us were enthused by them. It was like those elections for mayor in St. Louis. All the citizens preferred "None of the Above" but they could not get paid their four bits if they did not vote for the Democrat. Of our three options, the Yellow Creek Mine Road appeared the quickest path to relief. So we four reluctantly cast our lots in with those of the hucksters.

Eugene climbed back up and turned the rig about. To make up for the lost time, and to avoid the neighborhood's highwaymen, he snapped the team into a smart pace.

If you are the type of person who always reads the small print in a contract, you might say we contributed to our own peril. It is just like you might blame the residents of St. Louis for all their crooked mayors. Fred and Walter and Riley and I would not judge ourselves so harshly. For the trouble that soon overcame us, we would blame Kupperkeeper and Gould.

The coach was not on the Yellow Creek Mine Road for more than ten minutes before the pair were back to their old habits. They still were passing their own gab-gas because they liked the sound of it, but now they were pumping up the pressure because they knew the noise irritated us so much. I guess it was their way of showing that our threats did not intimidate them, and our comfort did not concern them.

Their talkatty-talk did not stop until the coach came over a blind bluff and hurried down a steep incline. At the bottom was a mire. And into this bog went team and stagecoach. The horses plunged into mud over their hocks and the coach was plugged in over its axles.

"Goddamnit! Goddamnit! Goddamnit!" cried Eugene. "Willis! Get them horses unhitched before they panic. Goddamnit!"

Kupperkeeper and Gould threw their door open but one look at the hip-deep muck convinced them to remain inside. The rest of us piled out the other door and waded into the soup to help Willis. If not quickly led to safer ground, the horses would injure themselves and maybe damage the wagon, too.

"Goddamnit! Goddamnit! Goddamnit!" repeated our driver. In a crisis, Eugene was a man of few words.

We led the nags to the dry bank about a rod from the sunken coach. Eugene and Willis calmed the beasts. The rest of us sat down to empty our boots of the water and mud.

"We're gonna have to team 'em up again and run a line to the wagon to pull it out," instructed Eugene.

"Will you need some help with it, Gene?" a voice called.

We turned about to find a man holding a repeating rifle. The gun was trained on us.

"Well, I'll be damned," said Eugene. "Is this your doing, Milton?"

"Aw, don't feel bad, Gene. I had you comin' or goin'."

Eugene spit on the ground. "Damn. I figured that oak was you. We should have just turned back. Damn."

"Now don't be hard on yourself. Anybody'd do the same."

"You got lucky on this one," said Eugene.

"Now, now, Gene. Give me a little credit here. I stumbled on this flooded spot and then I cut the tree. I fancied it was a pretty clever plan."

"Shit," observed Eugene. "They're gonna get you one of these days, Milton."

"I guess they will, Gene. But not today, huh? Who's your new man?"

Eugene introduced Willis and the four of us on the ground to Milton Sharp, and we saw for ourselves why he was called the Gentleman Bandit.

"I always like to know who I'm robbing," Milton told us. "You never know when we might meet up again and I'd like you to think we're friends."

Such politeness is not common among any of the thieves or highwaymen of my acquaintance, and I for one appreciated it. Milton inquired as to our occupations, where we were from, and what family we had. When he learned that we passengers were not presently employed he said, "I'll spare you boys your personal goods if there's anything worth taking in the safe box."

Although, he kept his rifle pointed in our direction all through the visit.

"There's two more fellas still in the coach," volunteered Eugene.

Milton said, "You don't say? Shy fellas, huh?"

We had to laugh at that one. Milton could not have known what we found so funny, but he laughed too. "I like you boys," he said. Then he shouted out, "Okay gents. You, in the coach.

Time to get a little wet. Come on out and please keep your hands up!"

"We ain't coming out," shouted Kupperkeeper.

Milton's face expressed amused shock. To us he said, "That don't sound too friendly." Toward the coach he hollered, "Now come on fellas. I ain't gonna hurt you. And I said 'please.'"

"We ain't coming out!" yelled Kupperkeeper.

Milton raised his rifle and fired a round in the air. "Get your asses out here or I'll fill 'em with lead!"

The coach door opened and out crept Kupperkeeper and Gould with their hands up. As they struggled into the mud, Gould's hat fell off and revealed his shiny head.

"Oh, my. You boys are dressed nice," Milton laughed. I'm sorry you gotta get dirty. You there! Baldy!"

"Me?" asked Gould.

"Yeah. Get up on board and get the safe box."

"Me?" trembled Gould.

"If you please. And if you think about the shotgun up there, it'll be your last thought. You understand me?"

Gould climbed up with some difficulty and grappled with the safe box. "It's lashed on," he lamented.

Milton sighed. "Well then, I guess I'll just have to shoot you and send somebody who can do the job."

Gould froze in sickly terror.

"You damn fool!" yelled Milton. "Unbuckle it."

"I'll try," said Gould.

"Thank you kindly," said Milton. To Kupperkeeper, he said, "You just stay where you are with your hands up. You're gonna need 'em in a minute here."

Gould managed to free the box and Milton ordered, "Hand it down to your friend."

"I won't be party to a robbery," objected Kupperkeeper.

"Gene?" asked Milton. "Am I being unreasonable?"

"You better do like he says," Eugene advised Kupperkeeper.

"Your role in this will be made known, Blair," said Kupperkeeper.

"Aw, to hell with it!" said Milton and he sighted the rifle at Kupperkeeper's head.

"Don't shoot!" cried the target. "I'll take it!"

Milton lowered the rifle. "Now, Baldy. Listen carefully and do all this real slow. Hand the box down to your friend."

Gould accomplished the task.

"Now real slow. Real slow, pick up the shotgun by the barrel and drop it into the mud."

Again Gould completed his assignment.

"Now there's another gun up there probably. Do you see it?"

"No," said Gould. "That's the only one."

"That true, Gene?" asked Milton.

"It's under the seat," answered Eugene.

"Baldy," Milton called to Gould. "I don't think you're cut out for this line of work. Look under the seat, get the gun and drop it over."

Once the second shotgun was safely sinking into the muck, Milton told both men to wade ashore and set the safe box at his feet. With a single well-placed bullet he blew the lock on the box. The noise almost caused Kupperkeeper and Gould to jump back into the bog.

Upon examining the contents he announced, "Well boys, this ain't bad. I won't need your own money. Keep it and tell your friends that Milton Sharp is an honest bandit."

This seemed a fair deal, but Kupperkeeper could not leave it alone. "We'll still see you hang, Sharp."

"Is that so?" said Milton. "And who might you be?"

"I am Ephraim Kupperkeeper and me and my associate are friends with the stockholders of this line and we'll see you hang. Mark my words."

"And your associate is Baldy here?"

"My associate is Mister Gould here."

"How do you do, sir," said Gould. "Only, I'm not really friends with anybody and I just met Mister Kupperkeeper here and he doesn't speak for me at all. Please sir, I don't mean no offense."

"Solomon, you coward ... " Kupperkeeper began.

"Don't be familiar, sir!" interrupted Gould. "I don't care what happens to Mister Sharp, and I don't know you from Adam."

"I always knew you were a lying bastard and now I know you're yellow too!" cried Kupperkeeper.

"You're a bigger liar than I am and you aren't half the salesman either!" retorted Gould.

"That's horseshit and you know it!" yelled Kupperkeeper.

"Shut the hell up!" Milton shouted. "The both of you!"

Milton carefully eyed the hucksters before continuing in a calm voice, "You boys are agents of some kind, huh?"

"That's correct, sir," piped in Gould all friendly. "I sell tunnel track and Mister Kupperkeeper sells hand tools, or so he tells me."

Kupperkeeper steamed right up. "You know damn well I do, and I out-sell you every year."

Milton cut them off, "Now boys, let's not argue over this stuff. Here's what you're gonna do. Your nice clothes have gotten all wet and muddy, I'm sorry about that. So I want you to please take them off, and your boots too."

I never thought I would see Kupperkeeper and Gould speechless, but this instruction did the trick. Finally Gould stuttered, "That's kind of you, Mister Sharp. But I don't mind the dampness. Not one bit. But thank you, sir. Thank you."

Milton said, "I don't want to put any holes in those expensive shirts of yours. So take 'em off. And please take off your boots and shake 'em out. Elsewise, I'm going to shoot you."

At first I speculated if the two would let themselves get killed rather than pony up the clothes. Then, slowly, Gould took off his shirt. Kupperkeeper removed his boots and a gold watch fell from them.

"You'll hang. Hang sure as sundown," said Kupperkeeper.

"There, there, my friend. You keep up this talk and sundown for you may not be sure at all. Oh my, I'd bet that watch is real gold. You're not done. Shirt and pants, if you please, and you, Baldy, off with the boots."

Off came Gould's boots revealing his watch and money belt. Kupperkeeper's money belt was plainly visible tied around his gut when he stripped off his shirt.

"Put the belt on the ground," said Milton. Then, "Thank you, gents," as he kicked the loot toward the safe box. "Now, walk back over there by the water. I don't want any stray bullets catching the gentlemen behind you."

"Ohmygawd," said Kupperkeeper.

"Oh, please. Oh, please. Please don't kill me. Please," blubbered Gould.

Eugene spoke up, "Milton, you've never hurt anybody before."

"That's true, Gene," said the bandit. "But my patience has never been tried in this manner. And I believe Mister Kupperkeeper truly would like to see me hung."

"Well, Milton," said Eugene. "You've always been very considerate every time you've held me up. I've tried to return the courtesy best I can. As a favor to me, I'd sure appreciate it if you don't shoot these fellas."

"I'll tell ya what, Gene. I don't think I owe you any favors. But you're a good man, so I'm going to let you line up your horses and get your wagon out of the mire. And while you're doing that, I'll think over what I'm going to do with these hucksters. I'll warn you though, I don't like either one of 'em too much. And I don't think they like me."

Eugene put us to work quickly and in hardly any time at all we had the wagon hauled to solid ground and the team hitched to go. All the cockiness was out of Kupperkeeper. He sat starring into the slime. Gould sat weeping with his head between his knees.

Eugene approached Milton Sharp. "Well? How is it going to be?"

"I don't want to make any more trouble than necessary for anybody," said Milton. "So you just be on your way."

Eugene asked, "Can those two get on board?"

"Oh, Gene. You know I couldn't ever shoot anybody if I didn't have to. But I think I'll let these dandies walk the rest of the way. It'll do 'em good. They can use the time to think over their manners. You boys won't miss them on the trip, will you?"

Eugene seemed satisfied. "Thank you, Milton."

"Don't mention it," said the highwayman.

Riley, Walter, Fred and I loaded into the coach and enjoyed a blissfully quiet ride all the way into Wellington.

I heard a posse went out looking for Milton Sharp. They found Kupperkeeper and Gould hiking in their underwear along the Smith Valley Road about twelve miles from the Yellow Creek Mine.

In one version of the story the pair were arguing up a storm about who was the better salesman. In another version, the two were not talking to each other at all. The facts of this story, as well as the moral of the thing, are points of much disagreement. However, the place where the robbery occurred came to be known as Hucksters' Mire. Everybody agrees on that. To this day you can still find it on any good honest map.

What became of Milton Sharp is another whole tale altogether.

* * *

# Brutus Blinkenberry
# Orders a Bride

If you jarred me out of my bunk in the midst of the night and asked if I ever consorted with management, I would promptly say, "Never! I'm a labor man through and through."

Any logical person would thus conclude that my knowledge of the higher-ups' personal lives would be minimal at the best. Certainly my familiarity with the domestic relations they maintain with their wives and sweethearts and such should be sorely lacking.

This is a fine example of the danger in waking a man in the midst of the night for purposes of interrogation. You won't always get the unblinking truth.

Be as skeptical as you want to be, but the fact is I once was quite the chum of a mine boss, and the most privy party to the intimate details of his courtship. I am not bragging about it. Nor am I making any soul-cleansing confessions. It is just one of those episodes that can befall a fellow when he gets a little careless with his principles or his associations.

In the years after the War, the Union's effort to pay for that sad struggle was keeping Virginia City slugging silver pretty near night and day. Work was plentiful and I found mine at a modest independent hole called the Rocky Path. One night, after I had spent a brutal day picking bedrock and then drinking a bootful of Hiram's Best, the mine's foreman shook me from my slumber.

"I want you to drive the rig tomorrow," he ordered. "We'll be collecting our new owner coming from Rochester. I'll be by before dawn. Be awake."

I cannot recall my exact reply. It was either, "Yes, sir! I'll be up and ready before the cock crows." Or it might have been, "Go bugger yourself, you lackey bastard." Nocturnal conversations, besides falling short of their reputation for total honesty, often squirm away from accurate reconstruction.

Whatever my answer of the night, the foreman presented himself bunkside an hour before the sun, and briskly mobbed me out of my dreams and into the stable to harness the rig. By the time we reached the Wells Fargo office, the sky was brightening. The same could not be said for my stagger-souped head. To my relief, there was time aplenty to coffee up my senses, and then sneak an eye-opener when the foreman visited the outhouse.

The night-run stagecoach from Reno was due sometime between six and seven o'clock depending on weather, highwaymen, disgruntled Paiutes, and other acts of God. It arrived without apology at the stroke of nine. A well-dressed but dust-creased man of perhaps twenty-five years sprung from his perch on the roof of the vehicle. Jumping sprightly to the ground and slapping the rump of the pivot horse in the same movement, he shouted up to the teamster.

"Well, George, that tumble was a cracker. But by shakes, what an adventure!"

This, I learned, was the Rocky Path's new lord and master, Brutus Blinkenberry, Esq.

"You sure you don't want a doctor to look at that wound, Brutus?" asked George.

"Great gluttony, no! It's only a bruise. Besides, I couldn't have taken it in any fleshier part, could I now?"

A terrified look of concern came over the foreman's face. "Were you injured, Mr. Blinkenberry?" he yelped.

"Call me Brutus, friend," came the open reply. "You'd think I would have been hurt when that branch knocked me off the coach, but I didn't suffer a scratch. What damage there is came later when the horse spooked and kicked me where I can't see. All's well that ends well. Coach intact. Horse intact. Brutus intact. Shaken, but all of a piece. Who are you, friend?"

The foreman introduced himself without acknowledging your faithful narrator and he recommended the services of one of Virginia City's more sober osteopaths.

As to the physician, Brutus said, "Wouldn't think of it. At least, not before I see my gold mine."

"Actually, sir," explained the foreman. "We pull more silver out of her than gold."

"Silver it is, then," laughed Brutus. "Frankly, I don't care if it's copper, tin or zinc. It's mine and I'm going to make something out of it. Hie thee and me to the bonanza!"

It took a while for the foreman to understand that Brutus wanted to proceed directly to the Rocky Path. Once that was firmly established, the three of us loaded the new owner's carpet bags into the rig and hied our way to the mine. Along the route the foreman and I learned more than we necessarily wanted to about Brutus Blinkenberry's history (both personal and family), his philosophies (both financial and social), and his professional ambitions (which were mostly lard-fried left-overs from the history and philosophy volumes).

Brutus was heir to the "infamous" Blinkenberry fortune of Rochester, New York. He did not explain why it was so infamous. It is not as if his family had made their money by selling maggoty meat or dud musketcaps to the Army of the Potomac or anything like that. His grandfather had earned the initial fortune by manufacturing friction matches. Then his father heaped up another pile by cornering the graphite pencil market in six states plus the Commonwealth of Massachusetts and the District of Columbia.

After studying the law at Yale College, Brutus decided he was tired of the "poses and pretensions and boiled shirts" of wealthy society. He bought himself an army commission and joined the staff of Secretary of War Edwin Stanton as an adjutant. Somehow this experience inflamed him with an awe for the "common working man" and when the War concluded he set his sights for the far West where I guess he thought he would find working men more common than those stuck east of the Mississippi.

To this end, he badgered his father to purchase "a little something on the frontier" and from the sound of it I reckoned the old man was glad to be rid of the boy. Mixed into the story somewhere was the notion that he was going to show 'em all what he could do by the sweat of his own brow and he would like to see the look on Rosemary Priscella duPont's face when she learns he has run off to the farthest edge of the civilized world and was not likely to return to New Haven alive. So here he was, the mint-new owner of the Rocky Path, bright eyes atwitter, jaw set boldly into the wind, and all in a lather to get his hands dirty.

"I want to get right into the bowels of the earth," Brutus told the foreman.

The foreman said, "Yes. I can see to that."

"But I don't want to be a bother to anyone. At least not to the honest laborers."

"Yes sir. I'll see that no one's bothered by you," assured the foreman.

"But the bigshots and presidents and major stockholders can beware. I know their game," Brutus continued.

"Unless I've been misinformed, sir, aren't you the only stockholder?" asked the foreman.

"I'm talking about the local gentry," said Brutus. "I'm their sworn enemy. I envision the Rocky Path Mine as a western beacon of egalitarian equality. A place where owner and worker can share a simple meal at the same table and afterwards shoot a game of snooker together in harmony and camaraderie."

"Snooker. Yes, sir. I'll see to it," noted the foreman.

For a short while Brutus rode in silence, perhaps contemplating all the frolicking good times in store for him over the billiard tables of his workers' paradise.

Then he said, "I won't need much of a staff. One aide-de-camp should do the trick."

"A what, sir?" said the foreman.

"An assistant. Preferably one who can read and write in English. Can you spare one good man?"

This gave the foreman pause. "I don't know offhand, sir, if we have anyone like that. We'll get one if you need one, of course."

"I'd rather it be someone presently employed with the mine. You can understand my thinking, can't you?"

"Oh, yes sir," the foreman lied.

"Surely there's somebody who can read."

"It's not just that, sir. The Path is a lean operation and all the men on the payroll have useful work and they're good at what they do ... not that being your assistant wouldn't be useful, I don't mean that. It's just that off the top of my head I can't think of anybody we could spare."

"What about him?" asked Brutus, and I felt a finger poked into my back.

"Him?" asked the astonished foreman. "You want him?"

"Can you read?" Brutus asked me.

"Yes, sir," said I.

"And write?"

"That too," I admitted — although I did not volunteer that penmanship was a skill infrequently called upon in Nevada and I had grown rusty in its practice.

"Oh, you can have him," conceded the foreman. "I was thinking of useful workers. You can have him starting now."

"Sold!" shouted Brutus. "The bugle sounds and our forces respond!"

Thus it came to pass that I was promoted from pickman to Brutus Blinkenberry's aide-de-camp, and the doors opened for all the entangled romantic heartache to come.

Upon arriving at the Rocky Path, Brutus had his first surprise. Staring in disbelief at the mine's shafthouse, he said, "This is it? Why, it looks like a factory!"

"Yes, sir," the foreman patiently agreed.

"Where's the hole in the ground?"

"That would be on the inside, sir."

"Of course," said Brutus, pleased that his mining knowledge was so rapidly expanding.

Hearing further conversation within the shafthouse was a chore due to the noise of the hoisting and pumping engines, and the clangorous labor of the carpenters, blacksmiths, and machinists.

"Amazing! Is the place on fire?" Brutus shouted while pointing to the bellows of steam shooting from the shaft mouth.

"No, sir. That's where we're going," said the foreman and he motioned toward the hoist lift that was barely discernable in the hot clouds. We called the lifts "cages" but they were not more than a frame with a floor. They were cages without bars and that is how we liked them.

Brutus seemed to pale some but quickly enough put himself back in command. "Yes!" he ordered. "Into the bowels!"

We approached the mainshaft and the foreman apologized that one of the two cages was temporarily on the blink. The operative cage had room for only two men if an ice barrel was going down and because an ice barrel was always going down, the foreman told me to wait for the next hoist. Brutus told the foreman that things were not going to work that way anymore. The aide-de-camp would ride with him and the foreman could wait.

"I'll be glad to wait," I yelled.

"No," voiced Brutus, "you're going with me." And that settled it.

The foreman firmly stated that in truth the aide-de-camp could conduct the tour as well as anyone and, if it pleased the owner, the foreman would just as soon get back to the regular business of the day.

Brutus said "Fine with me."

And the foreman said, "Suits me, too."

The exchange might sound civil enough when plainly recounted, but I knew that an owner going down the shaft without the foreman was a serious breech of mining custom and etiquette. Brutus, of course, didn't know anything. So in mindless defiance of tradition he pulled me into the cage with the ice and down we went toward the loading station on the main drift.

As we shot down the shaft he observed, "It's awful hot in here. What's wrong?"

"Nothing's wrong," I informed him. Then I quickly added, "Keep your hands and feet away from the sides." I was thinking how embarrassed I'd be if the new owner met his minions minus an arm or leg or noggin.

We stopped at the fourteen hundred-foot level and once again Brutus commented on the heat. "Hellifericious," he complained. "Can't we do something about this?"

"We'll go to the cooling room. It'll be better there," I said. "We'll deliver the ice."

Brutus seemed to be melting pretty fast so I transferred the barrel to a lumber cart and hurried him along the lateral tunnel to the cooling station under the blowing tubes. There he had the good sense to imitate the rest of us boys. He shed his shirt, guzzled water, and rubbed ice over his skin.

"Damn!" he said. "How does anybody get any work done?"

I advised him that the general practice was to dig for half an hour then rest for half an hour. This seemed to amuse him. "Sounds a lot like government work," he chortled.

The miners who overheard him did not seem to get the joke and Brutus did not notice his own cooling effect on the men. When we resumed the tour he asked me why the workers did not want to discuss much of anything. I gave the question some thought then I flat out fibbed to him.

"The boys are so awed and respectful of you that they can't think of anything to say."

"I can understand that," he said. "But I'll soon enough get to know what's on their minds."

"You can bet on it," I truthfully agreed.

The subject was abandoned as Brutus turned his attention to the marvels of a modern mine. He commended the profusion of candles and lanterns and asked if we'd ever had a fire. I felt obliged to tell him curtly it was bad luck to discuss that topic while underground. He was much impressed with the bright twinkling of the iron and copper pyrites in the mine's walls. He mistook the spectacle for nests of diamonds and was surprised to learn that all that glitters is neither silver nor gold, and most certainly not diamonds. The herds of rats which roamed the dig were not much to his liking, although he was pleased to hear the varmints ate well from the boys' supper scraps and rarely felt compelled to nibble on a miner. He examined the square-set shoring timbers, the ore chutes, the tunnel tracks, the giraffe cars topped out with the blackish-green raw ore of real silver, and down at the 2,000-foot level he briefly watched a crew sinking a new winze. It was at this lowest depth he burned himself twice. First he carelessly stepped knee deep into a stream of scalding ground water, then recoiled his naked back into a protrusion of hot quartz.

"I've seen enough of this hellbox," Brutus declared. "It must be three hundred degrees in here."

"Naw," I assured him. "It ain't half that."

"I think I want to look over the books now," was his only other opinion.

Following a lengthy respite in the cooling chamber we hopped aboard the hoist cage and returned to the topland world. We left the shafthouse (which seemed to hold no interest for Brutus) and I asked if he wished medical attention for his shin or spine.

He ignored my concern and said, "It's not much different than a coal mine in Ohio, is it?"

"I wouldn't know," I said.

"It's not what I expected," he told me. I thought I knew a bit how he felt. Most of us in Nevada have had our share of disappointments.

The man must have been licked to a frazzle what with the night-run coach from Reno and his rigorous tour of the Rocky Path, so I suggested we secure his lodgings. He was agreeable to the idea. We took the rig to the International Hotel where I deposited Brutus into the custody of a starched desk clerk and I spent the remainder of the day stationed at the Whiskey Trust Saloon.

In the following days I snuggled into the aide-de-camp duties as easily as feather into pillow. The job mostly consisted of driving Brutus here and yon in the rig, listening to his chilblained notions without comment of my own, and trying to spare him from head bumps and knee skins. In between these less than arduous tasks I was to keep myself available at the Trust. Early on it looked as if the vocation would strain my skills in neither reading nor writing, and might only be a test for my liver.

Brutus showed no inclination to return to the bowels of the earth. He made a few perfunctory examinations of the records on the company clerk's desk and provisioned an office of his own in a room above a barbershop on D Street. His most diligent activities were directed at establishing the Rocky Path as a western beacon of egalitarian equality, and determining which noses of the local gentry were ripe for tweaking. In both of these goals he proved remarkably inept.

You might think a bunch of raw miners would suck on to a visionary owner like piglets to sow teats. Brutus surely tried everything he could think of to make it so. He initiated a "study hour" after every shift. These purely voluntary sessions availed the boys to lectures by Brutus about the virtues of progressive labor relations. The boys chose not to avail themselves.

He moved the study hour to the supper break and supplied a free stew from Mrs. Hansen's eatery. The workers came out of the Path to get the stew, then immediately returned to the noisy shafthouse to eat it.

Brutus had a corner of a warehouse cleared and he installed a billiard table and three tables for poker. This proved popular for a day. Everybody stopped work and put the things to use. When the foreman explained the amusements were intended for recreation only before or after the shifts, the tables quickly fell into neglect and the billiard sticks disappeared.

Finally, Brutus announced an all-hands wage increase of fifty cents per day. This assuredly would have turned the tide of public opinion, except the owners of the V & T Railroad announced they would suspend the Rocky Path's shipments of kerosene, timber stock, machinery parts, lubrication, and ice if the raise went through. To keep the mine operating, Brutus backed off.

The men at the Rocky Path did not really have anything against Brutus. They just saw no reason to love him. And the more I saw, the more certain I became that love was all that Brutus craved.

Brutus' ambition to become the supreme nose-tweaker of Virginia City's high society was the rear-end aspect of his persona and harder to comprehend. As the cards fell, it did not matter a twit. All the fashionable folks out on the end of C Street ignored Brutus, and the former sourdoughs who had hit jackpots were too busy squandering their fortunes on liquor and knick-knacks to pay him heed. In two weeks it was clear enough to one and all that the man was a salmon swimming in a sand pile. But no one, including his aide-de-camp, cared enough to tell him so.

I will grant him this much: he never complained. After exhausting his best ideas toward the reformation of Nevada's social and economic structure, he took to speculating about the absence of any communication from Rosemary Priscella duPont.

"I can't understand why she hasn't written. Maybe the mail isn't getting through," he mused.

"Most of us got the same problem," I assured him.

"But Mother's letters have arrived regularly," he said.

"Most of us got the same problem," I said.

"Do you think Rosemary is just being stubborn and she's really worrying herself sick?"

"That's what it looks like," I told him.

"I won't harbor any folderol from the spoiled scion of an over-fed capitalist!" he declared.

"Nor should you," I agreed, even though I was not certain as to the meaning or morality of "scion."

"I'll just marry somebody else!" Brutus announced.

"That'd show her," I conceded, knowing full well that the prospect of obtaining a likely female for matrimony in Virginia City was laughable. There was no earthly reason to believe that Brutus' sudden interest in nuptials would lead further than the nearest saloon or last longer than a Mojave cloudburst.

How wrong I was.

Brutus set to work compiling an inventory of the town's potential breeding stock. In one of the mine's account books he told me to enter the name of all acknowledged local maidens. I wrote: Maidens = zero.

To this we added the names of known widows and every unwrinkled spinster. Still, the list was none too long. To give the catalog a respectable length, and for a touch of pepper in the pot, I appended the names of six or seven of Virginia City's more open-minded working ladies.

Brutus took an afternoon off and went-a-callin' on the slim flock. For one reason or another not a one of the gals measured up to his specifications.

He informed me, "I want a wife who'll thumb her nose at the frivolity of wealth and privilege. I want a woman who will trek barefoot across the Humbolt Basin if her husband asks her, and not care how big his diamond stick-pin is. I want a woman who will encourage her man to reach for the greatness of the ages while she soothes his furrowed brow and mends his longjohns. I want a woman fit for a hero!"

In the ledger I wrote: Women fit for hero = none apparent.

There the matter might have rested had not an advertisement in *The Territorial Enterprise* captured Brutus' attention.

---

**MATRIMONIAL NEGOTIATIONS
at a REASONABLE price.**

Gentlemen! Be rid of cold, lonely nights!
Christian WOMEN available!

Find HAPPINESS and satisfaction
in HOLY MATRIMONY!

You need not suffer any longer.

Correspond to Mrs. Elizabeth Albright,
Bliss Cottage, Quarry Street,
Philadelphia, Pennsylvania

**RESULTS GUARANTEED!**

White Christian men only.
**NO DRINKERS!**

---

That same afternoon Brutus entered negotiations. He dictated the following letter to me:

> My dear Mrs. Albright,
>
> Kindly inform me as to what procedures are required to secure your services as a matrimonial agent.
>
> This is a matter of some urgency.
> Address all correspondence to the care of the International Hotel, Virginia City, Nevada.
>
> Respectfully yours,
> Brutus Blinkenberry

"Do you want me to add the 'Esquire' to your name?" I asked him.

"Not on your life. I don't want to attract any gold-digging social climbers," he said.

To seal the deal, he told me to write:

> P. S. I attest to the truth that I am a sober white Christian. I always have been and I always will be.

We sent the epistle eastward via the good offices of the Overland Stage Company and awaited reply. My duties soon included the daily inspection of incoming mail at the V & T depot, both coach offices, and the new federal post office in the back of the Majestic Saloon.

Every day Brutus asked, "Anything come in from New Haven?"

Every day I answered, "Not a word. And nothing from Mrs. Albright, either."

An otherwise uneventful autumn passed.

In December, a letter arrived from Philadelphia.

Dear Mr. Blinkenberry,

CONGRATULATIONS! You have opened the door to a new and HAPPY life and can look forward to becoming a COMPLETE and BLISSFUL man.

You may rest assured that I will find a truly compatible mate for YOUR NEEDS and circumstances. You will SOON be a joyfully MARRIED man if you faithfully complete these five EASY steps.

Step 1. Post five American dollars ($5.00) in currency, coin, stamps, United States Bank cheque, or New York State negotiable bonds to: Mrs. Elizabeth Albright, Bliss Cottage, Quarry St., Philadelphia, Pennsylvania.

Step 2. Write and post to the above a description of your personal habits and financial prospects.

Step 3. Upon receiving correspondence from the intended bride whom I have PERSONALLY chosen for you, convey your HONORABLE intentions directly to her.

Step 4. Make the necessary financial and travel arrangements directly with your SOON-to-be bride.

Step 5. DO NOT BE UNTRUTHFUL! A happy marriage can NOT be based on deception or misrepresentation. YOU ARE LEGALLY LIABLE FOR ALL OF YOUR PROMISES.

I eagerly await your correspondence. The sooner
you complete STEP NUMBER ONE, the sooner
you will have a MATE FOR LIFE warming your
home and heart.

Most sincerely yours,
Mrs. Elizabeth Albright

Brutus allowed me to read the missive then instructed,
"When you write up this letter, do it on foolscap then copy it
down neat on the good parchment. And I don't want any ink
blots this time."

I had been practicing with pen and ink, so I was pretty sure
that I could please the boss.

"My dearest Mrs. Albright," he began. "Thank you for
answering the fondest hope of a man struggling alone to bring
enlightenment and utopian justice to the barbarian wilderness.
Enclosed you will find five dollars. Please send details about my
bride at your earliest. Yours in gratitude, Brutus Blinkenberry."

"That's it?" I asked.

"Should do it, I think," said Brutus.

"What about Step number two?" I chided. "I think you
got to follow the instructions or they're likely to ship you an
underpacked crate."

"Yes," he argued, "but look at Step number five. If I tell
the truth about myself I'll either get a fortune hunter, or one
of those stuck-up debutantes who flutter their eyelashes at the
coxswain of the Yale crew team every time an honest fellow
leaves the cotillion floor to get her a cup of raspberry punch!"

He had me with that one. I had not for a moment
considered the peril of an eyelash-fluttering debutante. "Well

then," I said. "Send it the way you got it. It's probably a pig in a poke no matter what you do."

Brutus thought my advice over, then asked, "If you were sending for a wife what would you say?"

"Me? How would I know?" I answered.

I did not tell him my honest view of the matter: Miners should not get wives or tattoos. Those sort of things may be fine for men, like sailors, who don't seem bothered by permanent attachments, but miners are a more transient lot. Miners are more suited to getting rich or getting drunk — both conditions, as far as I could see, being ones that quickly pass.

"Here's my thought," he persisted. "A woman who would settle for you would be a paragon of patience and faithfulness. Remember, I'm not shopping for a Josephine-in-the-court style wife. The East is crawling with them. I want more of a Rebekah-at-the-well kind of woman."

I exclaimed, "Ah!" And because Brutus thought so highly of my manly attractiveness, I decided to play along. "Okay then, what about adding this, 'P. S. I am an honest miner at the Rocky Path Mine in Virginia City. I gave up smoking cigars because they hurt my lungs. I get a tub bath every week. I don't have much money but someday I hope I'll have more. To my knowledge no decent man in Nevada has anything bad to say against me.'"

"Perfect!" Brutus approved. "That's the sort of testimony that should fetch up the salt of the earth, and it's nothing that I couldn't back up as my own in a court of law. Send it."

This I did. The letter was, after all, over the name of Brutus Blinkenberry and I foresaw no danger to myself of legal persecution or imprisonment under the conditions of Mrs. Albright's Step Number Five.

Throughout the winter all remained quiet on the New Haven front, but come March a shot was heard from Pennsylvania. A beautifully penned epistle arrived from Altoona. Brutus tore into the envelope like a hungry raccoon into a corn sack. I, too, was more than a little eager to see the yield — same as I'd be when any friend draws to an inside straight in a no-limit poker game.

Here is what was written:

> Dear Mister Blinkenberry,
>
> My name is Miss Gladys Beck. Mrs. Elizabeth Albright wrote me that you are a man looking for a good wife. I am looking for a husband.
>
> You should know that until March 31, 1865, I was engaged to Private John Stillman of the 198th Pennsylvania Volunteers. On that day my beloved John died in a place called Five Forks. On that same day, I also lost my brother Henry and my brother Samuel. I have properly grieved.
>
> I am afraid to travel to Nevada and marry a man I have never met. However, I will do this if you want me. Mrs. Albright says you are a well-groomed Christian man with no bad habits. She says you might be rich someday. I do not care about this. I only ask you to be as polite and faithful as you are able.
>
> I am a Methodist. I hope this does not trouble you. It does not trouble me. I think God is too busy to worry about Altoona. He let all the men get killed in the War.

I can work hard. I took care of mother and father
before they died. I took care of my brothers
before they left to war. Then I took care of the
farm.

I am 27 years old. Mrs. Albright did not say you
wanted a young woman, so maybe you will still
have me.

If you tell me to do so I will come to Nevada
and marry you. There is nothing to keep me in
Altoona except my own fear of going.

Sincerely,
Miss Gladys Beck
Beck Farm, East Road, Altoona, Pennsylvania


"Well?" Brutus put it to me. "What do you think?"

I inched my way into the problem, "Well, it's hard to say. You can't expect her to look like much. By that age they're usually worked half way to leather."

"That's only if they've delivered a brood or two. Isn't it? Besides, she's a farm girl and they're healthy as turnips. Aren't they?"

"Hardly a girl," I couldn't help emphasizing.

"I guess that can't be helped," he said.

I could see he had made up his mind.

He proclaimed, "She's neither socialite nor harlot. A man could not ask for much more than that. I'll take her."

Brutus ordered my pen unsheathed to shovel his bread upon the matrimonial waters.

Dear Miss Beck,

I am quite willing to pay for your transport to Nevada and marry you.

Enclosed you will find a cheque in the amount of $100 redeemable at the First Industrial Bank of Rochester, New York.

At your earliest, settle your affairs in Altoona and arrange transport to Virginia City.

It's not your fault you are a Methodist. It won't bother me as long as you only practice it in moderation.

Very respectfully yours,
Brutus Blinkenberry

Having penned the proposal, I was ready to call it a day and celebrate the blissful union from the comfort of the Trust. Brutus had no such ambitions. He told me to find a sheet of the Rocky Path's official business stationery and transcribe another letter. This one was addressed to Rosemary Priscella duPont of New Haven, Connecticut. Here it is as I verily wrote his every word:

Dear Rosemary,

Perhaps you will be surprised to hear that I am still alive. The dangers and tribulations of the West cannot be imagined by anyone who has not experienced them. Twice I have peered into the eyes of death.

Fortunately, I did not flinch and I survived, albeit with bodily scars. The first test came during the journey to Virginia City when I was attacked by wild beasts. The second, and far more terrifying, came 2,000 feet under the ground when an explosion of hell's fury impaled me upon a lance of burning rock.

My vision of a world where owners and laborers lie together as predicted for the lions and the lambs will begin here in this desolate place. Already I have awed the workers into a respectful silence. Soon I hope to earn the trust of these unfortunates so they will unburden their wretched miseries to me. Then, like your cousin Winfred who is having such success bringing the Faith to the heathen Chinese, I will raise their hearts and minds to the pinnacle of social enlightenment.

The local powers tremble at my sight. To my advantage, their fear has silenced them and I have been spared the aristocratic blathering so common at, let us say, your father's dinner table!

Please be advised that I am withdrawing my request for our engagement. I am soon to marry Miss Gladys Beck of the Altoona Methodist Becks. If you have anything more to say to me, you had best say it soon. Life is cheap here in Nevada.

As ever yours,

Brutus told me he would sign this letter himself, as well he should. It was a masterful yarn showing his ability to shine the facts into a blinding brilliance. If he wasn't already a mine owner he could easily find employment as a newspaper correspondent.

"That should roast her choker a little," he confided to me as he scrawled his John Hancock all across the bottom of the page.

We put both letters into the Overland's mail pouch and awaited results. In May, the good word came from Miss Beck.

> Dear Mister Blinkenberry,
>
> Thank you for your proposal of marriage. I accept. I appreciate the money you sent. It will help very much.
>
> I have arranged the sale of Beck Farm to my neighbor, Mister Grimes, who has helped me prepare for the trip.
>
> I am also selling all my useful possessions and house tools. It will cost too much to ship them. I think it proper that I arrive in Nevada with a dowry. It is modest but I am proud of it.
>
> I will leave Altoona on April 21. Mister Grimes tells me I will travel to Cincinnati and then to St. Louis. I will go to Kansas City, St. Joseph and Omaha. Mister Grimes is not sure where I will go after Omaha but he says I have plenty of money to get to California, if I wanted to. Once I went to Johnstown with my brothers but that is as far west as I have ever been before.
>
> Mister Grimes says that if God is willing I will get to Virginia City by the first week of June. I pray so.
>
> Dearly yours,
> Gladys Beck

On the same day that Brutus received Miss Beck's letter, the Rocky Path received a letter from the Newton & Sons Manufacturing Company of San Francisco confirming a shipment of elbow bracket bolts. Brutus placed both letters in a file marked "pending supplies" and did not make further comment.

During the remainder of May, Brutus grew noticeably edgy. It is no wonder. The suspense would gnaw at the nerves of any man. Each day as I returned to his office from my appointed rounds, he would ask, "Any word from Rosemary?"

"Nope." I'd say

"Are you sure?"

"Sure as I was yesterday," I'd tell him. "And by the way, your package from Altoona didn't show up either."

"The tides are ebbing," he'd philosophize.

On the first day of June, I think his brain finally snapped.

"I have been thinking deeply," he said. "Of all the explanations for her silence, only two make any sense. Either she is dead, perhaps from a boating accident on Long Island Sound, or, and this is the one I'm favoring, she is traveling to Nevada as we speak. What do you think?"

I thought the wrong answer could jeopardize my cushy aide-de-camp job, but that is not what I said, of course. Instead, I rubbed my chin and squinted one eye while rolling the other one. This gesture is much favored by the oldtimers in the Majestic Saloon when called upon for sage advice or opinion. Besides gaining time to collect a clever retort, the ruse convinces the audience that a fellow is giving serious consideration to the question.

"Yep," I said at last. "That would explain it."

Over the next few days Brutus vacillated between the Rosemary-is-dead and the Rosemary-is-winging-her-way-here theories. Which thought he held at any particular moment did not seem to matter. Both brought him immense pleasure.

On June 4, events began to catch up with the speculations. I rushed into Brutus' office and announced, "She's here!"

"Rosemary?" he shouted.

Damned if the boss did not have me stumped again. I had given no credence to his Rosemary-on-the-wing humbug, so upon hearing a woman had arrived on the Overland and was looking for Mr. Blinkenberry I concluded it was Miss Gladys Beck. I had not troubled to verify the goods.

This time I stuck to the truth, "I don't know, sir. I guess we should find her and find out. Huh?"

Brutus jumped from his seat and charged the door but at the stairs he halted abruptly. Turning back to me, he said, "It could be either one of them."

"Yes, sir," I agreed.

"You'd better come along. If it's Miss Gladys Beck, a chaperon would be correct. If it's Rosemary ... ah, women!"

Brutus did not complete the thought. He braced himself into a dignified stance and, like Daniel-into-the-lion's-den, he marched toward the Overland office with me trailing in his breeze.

The Overland man told us he had directed the woman to the International Hotel. No, she had not given a name. As to her appearance, he could only describe her as a "respectable lady."

We headed to the hotel. At the front door Brutus took a deep breath and bravely stepped toward his fate.

There was one woman in the lobby. Fittingly enough she was sitting in a love seat. Her back was to the hotel's saloon entrance and her eyes were on the front door. Her hands were folded in her lap and her high-buttoned shoes were tucked neatly beside a cowhide valise on the floor. She wore a black travel dress and a laced Amish cap with strings tied primly below her chin. She was not a great treat for the eyes of bystanders. She bore an unfortunate resemblance to Mrs. Abraham Lincoln, only not as sad looking, nor as crazy.

Brutus approached her, tipped his hat, and said, "Miss Beck?"

She stood up, not too far up because she was a slip of a thing, and said, "Mister Blinkenberry?"

"Yes. How do you do?" said Brutus.

"Fine. Thank you. How do you do?" she said.

"Fine. Fine," he replied.

They shook hands then stood looking at each other until Brutus thought to ask, "How was your trip?"

"Very long," she said.

"You weren't kicked by any horses were you?" he inquired.

For the first time she smiled. And my, it was a sweet smile. She had good teeth for a farm woman.

"No. I did not have the pleasure."

"It can happen," he said.

"I have no doubt," she answered.

For a moment conversation lapsed again. Then she said, "I brought you something." She reached into her valise and produced a small box bound with shop twine. Brutus accepted the box and starred at it as if she had handed him a lit hand-bomb.

"You may open it, if you wish," she told him.

He fumbled off the twine and pulled out a handsome porcelain shaving mug and a virgin new shaving brush.

She said, "The cup was father's. I purchased the brush in St. Louis."

A pained expression came on his face. "Uh. Thank you. This is ... generous."

"I shaved father and my brothers. They said I'm a very good barber."

Brutus kept his eyes on the cup and brush in his hands.

Normally I would be the last person to intrude upon the tête-à-tête of wooing sweethearts. In this instance I felt my office of aide-de-camp justified an interruption.

"Mister Blinkenberry has a gift for you, too," I said. "It's back at the office, but we'll deliver it this evening."

The interjection startled the both of them. Miss Beck recovered first.

"I don't believe I've met your friend, Mister Blinkenberry."

Brutus said, "Oh. I beg your pardon. This is my ... he's ... he's our chaperon."

"Chaperon?" Miss Beck marveled. "How very considerate."

"You must be tired after such a long journey," I suggested. "Maybe we should get you registered and you can rest."

"Yes," Brutus agreed. "That's a grand idea!"

I fetched Miss Beck's valise and we hustled her through the hotel's desk procedures. With promises to return in the evening for a late dinner, we stashed her in a room and retreated to Brutus' office for a man-to-man conclave.

"She's not what I expected," said Brutus.

"I can see that," I comforted. "But you're in it up to your eyebrows now."

"Yes. The wick is near the nub," he moaned. "Oh, Rosemary, Rosemary, why hast thou forsaken me!"

I resisted any observations about Brutus' own role in the drama and attempted to cast a ray of sun into his gloom.

"Well, you got yourself a dandy mug and brush set. I bet that brush cost three or four dollars in St. Louie."

"I wish she supplied the razor and strop. I could put them to good use," he whined.

As a general rule I am a great proponent for slipping out of any problem through the nearest door. In this instance, I thought fortitude might yet save the day, somehow, so I ignored his melancholy temper.

"We'll get you shaved before dinner tonight. Right now, I'd suggest we get her the welcome gift. I hate to be a nitpicker, but we should've thought to have a little something waiting for her. It's just plain courtesy," I preached.

Brutus plunged his face into his hands and groaned, "Forsaken and doomed. Done for like Ol' Abe."

While Brutus groaned, I was struck by dazzling ideas, "Maybe a nice teakettle. Do you think she'd like that?"

He reached into his desk and withdrew a ten dollar gold piece. "Get her anything you want. I need time to probe the depths."

I left Brutus to his depth probing and trotted off to purchase a keepsake for Miss Beck. A curious gaiety possessed me as I roamed the aisles of Haymaker's Merchandise Emporium. The shelves containing ladies' notions and household bric-a-brac were terra nova to me, but the exploration was a surprisingly pleasant one. I settled on a lovely ivory cameo with golden chain. Mr. Haymaker was most helpful and knowledgeable. He explained the bust painted on the cameo was that of Hestia, the ancient Greek goddess of the hearth. He recited,

> *Hestia, in all dwellings of men and immortals*
> *Yours is the highest honor, the sweet wine offered*
> *First and last at the feast, poured out to you duly.*
> *Never without you can gods or mortals hold banquet.*

I wrote the poem down and included it in the package that Mr. Haymaker wrapped with a yellow ribbon at no extra charge. A teakettle would have been more practical. But I liked the cameo.

When I returned to the office I found Brutus sweating over a letter he was composing to Rosemary.

"I can still see one way out," he explained. "If I can entice Rosemary out here, I can truthfully claim that I had proposed to her first. You see, I thought she was killed in a boating accident on Long Island Sound, which is also true, and it was then, in my grief, that I proposed to Gladys Beck. The whole thing is a dreadful mistake, but there's nothing to be done about it except marry Rosemary and send Miss Beck back to Altoona. I think it could hold up in court if we get the right judge."

"You're the lawyer," I said. "My advice for the here and now is that we get a bath and a shave, then take Miss Beck to a feed at the hotel's dining room."

Brutus frowned. "What for?"

"Look at it this way," I advised. "If you're trying to hold her off until Rosemary gets here, you don't want to get her suspicions up. I can't think of a better way of keeping the lid on than over a few thick beef steaks and some rhubarb pie at the International."

Brutus reluctantly saw the good sense in my strategy and the both of us went downstairs for a scrub and a scrape. During the tonsorials he warmed up to the evening's plan. He said, "Keep the banter on the light side. The weather is a safe topic. And plenty of emphasis on blizzards and droughts might help. Another good idea is to impress her with the rampant violence and drunkenness in Virginia City. Any other subject, especially anything about me, should be left alone, or at least vague. It probably won't be helpful telling her how Methodists aren't much welcomed here. I think Methodists already know as much."

With all this plotting, Brutus neglected to ask about his welcome gift to Miss Beck, and I neglected to remind him.

At the hotel the tryst started off satin smooth. All through dinner Miss Beck let the conversation follow any path Brutus wandered. Mostly it sounded like this,

Him: "In winter it gets frightful cold here."

Her: "I imagine it does."

Me: "Frightful."

Him: "Then summer comes and you near die from the heat."

Her: "That's so true."

Me: "Deadly heat."

Him: "Does it get cold in Altoona?"

Her: "It gets break-your-bones cold."

Me: "You don't say."

Him: "Hot too?"

Her: "Hotter'n the dickens."

Me: "Oooo, that's hot!"

This style of repartee held us through the main course but come the rhubarb pie, Brutus and I began to dry up. I was saving the gift from Haymaker's for just such an occurrence.

I placed it on the table and said, "Mister Blinkenberry got this for you. I hope you like it."

She untied the ribbon and carefully folded it before she opened the box. For the longest time she held the cameo and gazed on Hestia's image without speaking. Still, I could tell she was pleased because that tender smile returned, and any resemblance to Mrs. Lincoln just faded away. Silently she read the poem, then said, "I have never received anything so beautiful. Thank you."

That seemed to be the capper on the evening. Afterwards, as we polished off the rhubarb pie, we adopted the smile and nod form of togetherness. My grin felt lightheaded, although I'd only had two or three ryes. Miss Beck's smile looked grateful and endearing. Brutus' smile looked like his teeth were fused into a lockjaw.

After dinner we walked her up to her room. At her door she said to Brutus, "Until tonight, my only thought was how difficult and frightening this all is for me. I wanted to hurry and have it all done with. I never considered that perhaps you are frightened too. I see now, Mister Blinkenberry, that time may be on our side."

Brutus stood there mute as a mudcake.

"Good night, gentlemen," said she.

"Good night, Miss Beck," I said.

She went into her room and the instant the door closed Brutus hissed, "What in hell did you put in that note? And why in God Almighty's name didn't you get her a teakettle?"

"Well, sir," I said. "It was just some ditty that Mr. Haymaker suggested. The teakettle didn't seem like such a good idea because she hasn't any stove to cook it on."

This explanation sounded logical to me, especially considering I had invented it on the spot. The truth was, I did not know why I had done what I had done. Brutus was not noticeably mollified.

"If you're going to be so indegoddamdependent, I'll send you back to the bowels!" were the very words he hissed.

His threat was a serious one. Still, it did not dampen my frivolous mood. A mysterious giddiness had overtaken me. Threats could not lessen it. Liquor could not explain it.

In the days following Miss Beck's arrival, my general bliss continued despite the growing black humor in Brutus. Any remaining interest he had in the Rocky Path, its men, or Virginia City's high society evaporated like the desert dew. His hopes rested solely on incoming stagecoaches and mail. His fears were fixed on the nightly dinners we shared with Miss Beck.

I, too, began to share the boss' irritation with Rosemary's stony silence and unexplained absence. My spirits, however, were always high for the evening meal.

After a few days our dinner table conversations had thoroughly covered the climatic conditions and misdemeanors of both Nevada and Altoona, as well as other geographic statistics, and Miss Beck broached the subject of a wedding date. Brutus explained that he favored a proper period of chaperoned engagement, but perhaps the details of the arrangement could be discussed toward the end of the month. Later, Brutus told me that I was to remain at his side night and day, lest he accidentally run into Miss Beck alone and scandalize the community. Miss Beck had said that time was on their side. I began to wonder.

On the following Monday, the suspense ended. The letter from New Haven was on rose-colored stationery and the ink was purple. It was what we neither expected nor wanted.

Dearest Brutus,

How delightful to hear from you! Your sudden departure was all the talk for a fortnight. You might be relieved to know that I told our friends you were dispatched on a secret state mission by President Grant. To spare yourself any embarrassment I suggest you confirm this explanation if you ever return.

The West sounds dreadful. I'm sure you are enjoying it to the fullest. You should be interested to know that my cousin Winfred is no longer in China. Having decided the Chinese are incorrigible, he moved his mission to the Fiji Islands to labor among the cannibals. We will miss him of course, but it was his own decision. You may draw whatever moral you choose from this.

Father was surprised you are still alive. I need not quote him. Suffice it to say that his memories of you remain vivid. Please accept my deepest congratulations for your announced engagement to Miss Beck of the Altoona Becks. We are not familiar with her family but I'm sure they are well regarded in Altoona.

Please be advised that I, too, am engaged. The wedding will take place on the twenty-ninth of June. I am sure you remember Thaddeus Lowell Tyler. He brilliantly coxed the Eli crew to their win over Harvard in '64. Thaddeus forwards his heartiest sentiments to you, as ever.

Should you be unable to attend, you may forward the wedding gift to Father's cottage in Newport. Where might Thaddeus and I send our gift to you and Miss Beck?

With fondest regards,
Rosemary

Brutus let the letter drop to the ground. Then his arms dropped like dead weights. He slumped back into his chair.

"Thad Tyler," he mumbled, and gazed vacantly at the ceiling.

"This is not good," I said.

"Thad Tyler!" Brutus yelled. "That salt-logged pipsqueek! It's dirty business. That's what it is. Dirty business!"

Trying to ease the tension I said, "I take it this fella is a sailor."

"Thad Tyler!" he repeated.

"I bet he's got tattoos from stem to stern," I offered in the hope it would console the man. My words must have rekindled his old fire.

"There's still time to save her," he announced. Looking at his pocket watch he said, "I bet I could still get a coach to Reno."

"What'll I tell Miss Beck?" I asked.

"Tell her anything you want. Tell her I've gone to the Fiji Islands to save the cannibals!" With those words he was up and gone. It was Brutus Blinkenberry's last order to his aide-de-camp.

My first impression of the news from Rosemary had not been favorable. I was saddened. It looked like her engagement to Thaddeus Lowell Tyler would force Brutus into the arms of Miss Beck. With the boss beating a hasty retreat to the east, my opinion changed. I was happy. It seemed like a problem that, with fortitude, might still be resolved.

I went down to the barbershop and scrubbed myself to the bone. Then I had myself shaved, twice. I returned to my boarding house, put on my best clothes, stopped for a quick one at The Trust, and then went to break the tragic tidings to Miss Beck. On the way to the International I stopped at Haymaker's Merchandise Emporium and purchased a spanking new lady's handkerchief. I suspected she would need one.

She received me in the hotel's sitting parlor. To my relief we were alone. She did not appear unduly surprised that I was calling sans a Blinkenberry.

"Miss Beck," I began. "I have very bad news. Mr. Blinkenberry sends his respects and affection. Due to unforeseen urgent business he had to leave Nevada very suddenly."

I had the hanky at the ready but she did not need it as yet. "Will Mr. Blinkenberry be returning?" she asked.

"I'm afraid that he probably won't. You see, President Grant has sent him on a secret state mission to the Fiji Islands."

"Is that what he told you to tell me?" she asked.

"More or less," I said.

"Is it the truth?" she said.

"No," I told her.

"Thank you," she said.

I pulled out the hanky and was ready to sop up the tears. None were forthcoming.

She said, "I think I understand."

This next part was harder for me to say but I pressed on. "I don't know if Mr. Blinkenberry left any money for your return to Altoona. I don't have a lot, but if you want to go back I will help you."

She said, "That's very considerate. Thank you. But I have some money of my own."

Now I got to the hardest part of all. I said, "Miss Beck, I know you came here to marry Mister Blinkenberry and I'm sure this is a great disappointment. I have had disappointments here, too. I think all of us have."

"Yes. I have seen that," she replied.

I pressed on, "But if maybe you're thinking you don't want to go back, I can only say I am just a miner. And I'm not a Methodist. In fact, I'm not much of anything when it comes to religion. And I maybe drink a little. But I don't smoke cigars and I try to stay clean. I work hard when I have to. If you ask anyone about me, I don't think they'd have anything bad to say. I try to be honest. So, if you want to stay ... maybe ... if you wouldn't mind ... maybe ... you and I ... "

Miss Beck was silent. I hoped she understood me, or maybe I was afraid she understood me perfectly. She certainly was thinking deeply about something.

At long last she smiled her smile. I liked that. Then she spoke, "You are kind. Was it you who chose the cameo and the poem?"

"Well, I guess I did."

She gave the matter some more thought and then said, "I've come to the opinion that in Nevada, people are here to find what they want. In Altoona, people settle for what they have. I am in Nevada now. There is nothing left for me in Altoona. I am here to stay."

My hopes went up.

Then she continued, "As to your offer, I am touched and I appreciate it. But, no. Not now."

My hopes went down. I said, "Well, then. I understand." Then, though she did not need a handkerchief at all, I gave it to her anyway. "I bought this for you."

"Thank you," she said. "It's pretty as can be."

We said goodbye. She stayed sitting in the parlor with her thoughts. I went over to the Trust.

That was in 1870. Over time, Miss Beck established a clean and respectable boarding house of her own. For business reasons she called it "Mrs. Beck's," and she prospered. When the Great Panic hit in 1877, and Virginia City nearly went belly up, she started a free soup kitchen and fed every hungry miner, Paiute, and Chinaman in Storey County. When she passed away in 1904, the Methodist church could not hold half the men who showed up for the funeral.

To my knowledge, Miss Beck never got married nor got a tatoo. I never did either.

* * *

# How Rutherford B. Grutt Almost Lost an Ear in Hiko

To Me belongeth vengeance and recompense," sayeth the Lord. Of course, we all understand that He was referring to the absolute, eternal, and slow-to-get-here varieties of vengeance and recompense. The Lord will always send the right man down the river clanking the ankle irons into foreverish, but the process usually takes awhile. If you are not particular about the absolute and eternal requirements, and want your vengeance and recompense quick, you just couldn't poke under a better rock than a Nevada mining camp.

As evidence of this contention I offer Hiko, a rude little southeast hamlet in the district that eventually became Lincoln County. Hiko is squatted flush to the White River where the Sheep Mountains wear themselves out into the Pahranagat Valley.

Nothing much ever happened out that way unless you want to count the boulders that could roll uphill or the Delamar Dust that killed five hundred Mormon miners. By nothing much happening, I mean the neighborhood never produced enough gold or silver to interest the Eastern newspapers, so you probably never heard of it.

Don't ask me why I found myself there because I could not honestly tell you, except to say I was younger then and did not know pyrite from a pitchfork. I can remember it was a rugged hot summer in 1857, or maybe '59, and I thought a man could get rich by panning and placer mining. Well, I told you I was young.

I arrived with one horse and a mule, six dollars, and enough grub to last a month on my own. The spine saving blessings of a long-tom sluice were still books on the shelf to me, but no matter. If ignorance were an impediment to enterprise, Nevada would still be in the hands of the Indians.

So with pan in clutch I wandered to an uninhabited section of stream bed about three miles north of the settlement and proceeded to get my feet wet. In the first week I knew my fortune was made. Every panful of sand yielded a drag winking and blinking, and I packed the gleanings into a leather pouch until the thing was almost too heavy to carry. In the second week I went down to Hiko to cash the cache and was more than a little disconcerted to learn that I owned eighteen pounds of mica with a total dollar value of piddle on the open market.

After enduring the good-natured ridicule of my compatriots, I disregarded their advice to purchase a supply of mercury with which to separate gold from gangue, and went back to my stream.

In the third week I returned to town and bought the recommended quicksilver.

Then I staked a claim along a waterway that was crawling with all the rest of the greenhorns. By common consent every miner was allowed one hundred feet of riverbank to call his own. I called my stake, "The Golden Dream." I clearly posted the plot with large signs in accordance with local custom, and filed the claim with the district recorder.

After that, things got better, but not by much. I earned about enough to keep myself in beans if I sold the horse, which I did. And I still regret it.

I am loathe to burden you with these details of my youthful follies but it is necessary to smuggle in a lesson you won't pick up from *McGuffey's Reader*. Unlike the domesticated civilizations in San Francisco or Sacramento, out on the rough edges from Dogtown to Dollarsville, a man's staked claim and a man's horse still mean something. Neither of these possessions are likely to be of great value to the rest of the world, but to us miners they're more serious than Sundays.

After two months participation in the scraping of the stream we now called Wet Wool Creek, I felt like one of Hiko's founding fathers and assumed a fairly regular chair at Jess Samson's Saloon. It was here, in that hot summer of 1857, or '59, that I was introduced to the subtle complexities of Nevada justice.

I had knocked off work at mid-day because the sun was strong and my thirst was great. When I walked into Samson's I could plainly see that some manner of profound civic business was being undertaken. Jess Samson, the bald and bearded proprietor of the establishment, sat behind a couple of sawhorses with a board propped betwixt them. In his left hand he held a Bible and in his right hand he held a ballpeen hammer that he was banging on the plank in front of him. Standing before both Jess and sawhorses was Nate Bailey.

"No, no, no, no," Jess bellowed. "The court finds this potential juror is unfit because he owes Rutherford money and therefore ain't likely to be fair and impartial. Take him out and hang him."

"What?" exclaimed Nate.

"Aw, Nate. I'm only joshing you," said Jess.

"That's good, Jess," Nate laughed. "Because I'm sure you haven't forgotten that I owe you money, too. If you hung me, you'd slim down the chance of ever collecting it."

Jess scrutinized Nate with a newfound respect. "You have a sharp legal mind, son. Ever been in a trial before?"

"Hell, yes! Back in Scranton they used to haul me into court most every Monday morning for one damn thing or another."

"Good. Nothing's better than experience. The court appoints you the temporary prosecuting attorney for today only."

"Thanks, I guess," said Nate. "Any pay in it?"

"Naw," answered Jess. "But I'll give you one gratis drink."

Nate thought this over, and then said, "Well, I ain't never drunk gratis before. Is it anything like brandy?"

"You get one drink of anything you want free of charge," Jess explained. "'Gratis' means free in lawyer lingo."

Nate sincerely appreciated this lesson in jurisprudence. "I'll take it!" he said. "What do I got to do?"

"You prove that Rutherford is telling the truth and Lightload is lying. You also got to make sure that Vail gets hung fair and square."

Nate seemed pleased with the assignment and showed most of his surviving teeth in a grin. "Hell, yes. I think I can do that."

If you are puzzled by these proceedings, don't feel badly. I was mystified myself at first. It's what the legal minds call *in medias res*. It is rather like stepping blindly off a cliff into a pool of quicksand. You're not sure how you got there. You don't know how deep you're going to sink. And nobody can tell you if you're ever going to get out.

Jess hit his hammer on the board a few more times then called out, "Who's next?"

Although I was but a callow youth, I had enough sense to weasel toward the rear extremes of the crowd.

"Come on, boys," Jess pleaded. "We only need but one more juror and a lawyer for the defense. Any volunteers?"

Most of the men in my eyeshot took to examining the ceiling of Samson's Saloon.

"This won't take us long. You'll be able to see the hanging and get back to your business before sundown." Still, no one stepped forward. "All right. This court will just have to ad-hoc-eye two of you."

Jess perused the assembled crowd and then pointed his hammer at Bernhard Klok. "Bernie," ordered Jess. "You are hereby appointed attorney for the defense."

"I object, your honor," said Nate. "Klok can't barely speak English. Are we going to have to hold these trials in the Dutch lingo?"

The boys all laughed and clearly sensed that the prosecutor was one shrewd barrister.

"What do you care counselor?" Jess asked. "You're on the other side. Objection overruled. Bernie, step forward. Bernhard? Get up here!"

Bernie didn't seem to fully appreciate the prestige of his newly attained office and tried to exit himself from the saloon. His egress, however, was blocked by the amused miners at the swingdoors and they ushered him down to a seat of honor.

Because all this legal dickering had not slaked my thirst any, I used the Klok diversion to sidle up to the bar and try to get myself a stroke of the tonsil paint. For someone devoted to the facile anonymity of a mob, this was a misguided maneuver.

"You there!" the judge called out.

I was concentrating on getting the attention of the barkeep and hadn't the least suspicion that his Honor was addressing my skinny and naive self. Only when the other miners cleared a space around me as if I had the pox did I clever up to the subpoena.

"You! You, boy!" Jess repeated. "Do you know Rutherford B. Grutt?"

Caught with neither whiskey nor alibi at the ready, I fell upon the last resort of all fools and told the truth. "No, sir," I said.

"Are you familiar with Lightload Harry?" inquired his honor.

"No," I had to admit, still keeping along the veritas path.

"Have you ever had business with a man calling himself L. B. Vail?" the judge asked.

"Never heard of him," I honestly replied, and I was getting confident that my apparent failure in the examination might excuse me from further entanglement. I was disabused of this fantasy when the judge showed himself pleased as pickles with my innocence.

"The lad doesn't know any more than a half-wit," he proclaimed to the courtroom. "He's the best juror of the bunch. We can get started now. Court's in session." Jess then gave the table a triple whomp of abuse with his ballpeen and everyone rushed to get a good seat or a drink.

Given a voice in the matter, I would have preferred to go gratis. But like Bernhard Klok, I was escorted to center stage where I joined the eleven other collared citizens who had answered the call of jury duty.

Upon taking my place amidst this august body, Hal Steiner informed me that he was the jury's foreman and would tell me everything I needed to know and do. Guided by Hal's expertise, I got my first gander at the other principals in the litigation and learned what chicanery was afoot.

According to Hal, Jess Samson ran the most efficient and legal-like courthouse in all of Nevada. The present proceedings were a shining example. We jurymen would be adjudicating not one but two trials. The first would be a claim-jumping dispute involving one Rutherford B. Grutt who maintained that one Lightload Harry had repeatedly and nefariously dipped his pan into Rutherford's hunk of Wet Wool Creek. The second trial would be a capital crime affair to judge the destiny of one L. B. Vail who stole horses and murdered his accomplice, one Bob Knox. Vail was not on trial for murder because the whole community was relieved to be rid of one Bob Knox, but the horse thieving charge was serious and required our wisest judgment in weighing all the possible forms of punishment.

Hal was much impressed with the time saving benefits of conducting the two trials more or less simultaneously. "As long as we're blasting one hole, we might as well blow them all," he sensibly observed.

The Grutt versus Lightload litigation would open the docket because Jess Samson expected it to be the more complicated of the two, and therefore demanded some semblance of sober deliberation. The Vail matter had a more open and shut nature, so the clear-headed attention of the jury was not imperative.

Having been apprised of the *res* that I had missed before the *in medias* came along, I took to examining the contestants. Lightload Harry was perched in a chair next to Bernhard Klok. If a man's guilt or innocence can be read from his eyes, Lightload would confound any jury in the land. His right eye was normal enough and actively bounced around its socket in response to spoken word or sudden movement. But his left eye was a geechy thing stuck in its gaze to the middle of his face. So half of the time he looked half cock-eyed, and the rest of the time he looked completely cock-eyed. This cross-eyed aspect of his demeanor, although distracting for any observer, was only part of the conundrum. Lightload exhibited a hail-fellow-well-met joviality more befitting a politico stumping for office than a man on trial for grave offense. He said to Clem, "Howdy, Clem," and waved grandly. "Howdy, Merle," he said to Merle. "How-de-do, Hal. Hot day, ain't it?" he greeted our foreman. If anything, Lightload appeared to enjoy the attention bestowed upon him as one of the vaudeville's headliners.

Sitting adjacent to Lightload Harry, and manacled in chains hand to foot, was L. B. Vail. If you had yourself a poisoned well or a violated daughter and were seeking the perpetrator, you could not find a better-looking candidate than L. B. Vail. I cannot speculate upon what hogwallow had coughed up this razorback, but it would not be a place you'd want to visit after dark. He must have weighed near a quarter ton and his unbarbered grime-sodded black head-hair probably added a pound or two to that. A nasty scar meandered from his ear to the tip of his chin and his gnarled nose festered red with a field of whiskey daisies. He maintained an impolite glare at the court's presiding officer and obstreperously conveyed an attitude akin to a grizzly housed in a bullpen. From the hoofs up he was a gutter-dragged hirsute devil who wore his anger ire-side out, and plenty of it.

These observations are only meant to give you a fair and unbiased picture of the man. I formed no prejudicial opinions of the villain, although my fellow jurors were less impartial in their expressed convictions. Hal Steiner may have captured the panel's consensus when he stated his hope that "... the fat bastard won't break the rope when we dangle him."

Bernhard Klok, the freshly appointed public defender, completed the team at the defense table. Hal scooped me the information that Bernie was an odd bird who had arrived in Hiko some six months back with two burros loaded down to a kneebend. One of Bernie's burros carried the usual paraphernalia of a sourdough's trade. The other animal creaked under the weight of hundreds of books. Hal would not have believed this phenomenon had he not witnessed it himself.

Books! And the episode seemed all the more amazing because every one of the damned things was printed in German so any possible worth of the tomes, except to exercise the might of the burro, escaped the other miners.

Bernie's remaining idiosyncrasies were easier to understand. He tended to start work earlier than anyone else, kept at it longer, managed to coax a bit more gold out of Wet Wool Creek than the rest of the boys, and generally kept to himself. His ability to speak English, although tending toward the fractured and convoluted direction, was not as obscure as Nate Bailey would have you believe.

Over on the prosecution's table Nate was already enjoying his gratis drink and was busy exchanging confident banter with Rutherford B. Grutt. By any measure Rutherford would strike you as a real gentleman, so he was by far the strangest sight in Samson's Saloon. One look at the man and you just knew he had bathed that morning and was an odds-on bet to soak in a sudsy tub again that night. He wore a beaverskin stovepipe hat that was brushed and groomed to a twinkle. Any self-respecting beaver would probably jump into the trap if it knew its hide would end up in a fez like Rutherford's. His face was shaved smooth, save for a thread of mustachio etched above his upper lip, and I'd bet his cheeks were not strangers to talcum or Bay Rum. His green frock coat was perk as a rosebud, and you could look all you wanted at his cream linen shirt or black string tie or golden silk vest, and still not get a hint as to what he'd eaten for breakfast. Based on the impeccable cut of his presence a jury of his peers would be hard pressed to resist voting Rutherford all he was asking for, and then some. Only thing was, we dirty-nailed miners were not nearly the peers of such a fine specimen of genteel humanity like Rutherford, and we knew it.

Jess Samson brought the proceedings to the brink of order with a few judicious bangs from his hammer and called out, "All right, let's get a witness up here and find out what happened."

Nate Bailey stood up and said, "Yer honor, near as I can tell we got us two witnesses. One of 'em, Mr. Grutt here, will be telling the truth and the other, Lightload Harry over there, will be lying. So I propose we hear the truth first."

"All right," said Jess. "There being no objections to that, I don't think, the court calls Mr. Grutt to get sworn and tell his side of it."

The bell had rung on our little contest and we adjudicators leaned back in our chairs, bit off a chaw or two, and readied ourselves to sort out the bogus from the bunkum.

Rutherford marched straight up to Jess, reverently placed one hand on the Holy Book, raised the other toward heaven, and looked boldly into the faces of the jury. He gave us a smile that caught the reflection of the sun and, just so we'd know that he'd be letting us in on the inside track, he winked at us.

"Do you swear to tell the truth, the whole blasted truth, and nothing else but the truth, so help you God?" intoned Jess.

"Yes, your Honor, that I will. I swear to God," said Rutherford, putting plenty of ginger and honey into the swear-to-God part.

"All right," said Jess. "Sit down and get on with it."

"Thank you, your Honor. And thank you, gentlemen of the jury, for allowing me the privilege of seeking justice in this unfortunate matter."

Rutherford was just starting to describe the location of his claim, which he called the Velvet Eldorado, when Clive Livingston, the camp's carpenter, came barging into the proceedings bedecked with saws, planes, drills and vices, and an armful of planked timber.

"I don't think it's fair for me to be missing the trial, Jess," Clive announced. "I'm doing the work for nothing. I think I oughter be able to see what's going on."

"We ain't got to Vail's trial yet, Clive," Jess told him.

"I won't pay no mind to that," said Clive. "Once I get started, I don't want to move the work 'til I'm done. So why can't I just set up in here? That way I won't miss nothing, but the job will still get done."

Without further evidence I was in the dark as to Clive's mission, but it all seemed reasonable to Jess who after a Solomon-like pause for contemplation said, "All right, go ahead. But try not to make too much noise if you can help it."

Much pleased with the court's decision, Clive said, "Thanks, Jess," and immediately set up shop for the sawing and hammering that quickly enough followed.

"As I was saying," continued Rutherford. "My claim is validly staked and recorded, and my signs are posted in red paint on both my north and south perimeters on the creek."

"Just tell the boys what you saw Lightload do," chimed in Nate. He had moved well past his gratis drink and was fueling himself into a real warmth for lawyering.

"I'm getting to that. Thank you, Mr. Bailey. It was on the morning of July twenty and one, just after sun up. I saw Lightload Harry panning in my stake at least forty feet over the borderline. I admit, Harry's stake is just south of my own. Well, I thought, anybody can make a mistake once. So I didn't shoot him."

"That's a sign you are a fair and forgiving man," Nate said to Rutherford, but Nate was looking directly at us jurymen when he said it. "Go ahead with your story."

"But no man can say that Rutherford B. Grutt is a fool, so I kept a lookout and on July twenty and three, just at the light of day, I saw him again panning away plunk in the middle of the Velvet Eldorado. I was thinking to myself, this is too much! But I didn't shoot him again!"

"Why not?" Nate asked.

"Because I didn't have my gun with me at the time," answered Rutherford.

"And that was lucky for Harry, I'd say," said Nate. "And I think you boys in the jury would agree to that. Then what happened?"

"The next morning I was ready for him and sure enough, there he was, panning his way through my stake and heading toward Jess Samson's stake to the north."

"Wait a minute! He was heading toward my stake?" Jess exploded.

Rutherford was slithering into an answer for his Honor but Clive had chosen that moment to start hammering two boards together and the noise drowned out the reply.

Jess hammered back and said, "Hold on there, Clive. We're getting some important testimony now."

Clive paused and Rutherford continued with a happy smirk. "Yes, your Honor. Seems like my gold wasn't enough for him and he was going after yours, too."

"Well, I'll be," said Jess. "Imagine that! So, why didn't you finally shoot him?"

"Oh, I shot at him, your Honor. But the light was none too good and I missed him, and he skedaddled back to his own stake."

"Jess?" said Clive. "I can't do this work and not make a little racket. Can I get on with it?"

"Sure, go ahead. I heard all I want to hear." Then turning his attention back to Rutherford, Jess said. "That's one of the most amazing stories I've ever heard, Mr. Grutt."

"Your Honor, it almost makes a man lose faith in his neighbors, don't it? But I want all you gentlemen of the jury to know that I'm not one of those small-minded rascals who thinks one rotten apple spoils the whole barrel. You boys are all right by me, and I want you to know it."

We gentlemen of the jury almost did not hear Rutherford's benediction to us because of all the wood and nail clamoring by Clive. But we weren't yet half sauced, and Clive was only working half fast, so we heard enough of it.

Rutherford concluded his testimony with a grand and noble summation. "Now, I'm not a vindictive man, and you don't have to hang Harry or cut off his fingers or nothing like that. I think it would be a fair punishment, and a warning to all cheaters, if Harry just forfeited all rights to his claim and cleared out of Hiko."

"And what might this court do with the claim after we take it from him?" Jess asked.

"Well," Rutherford replied. "It seems like I'm the aggrieved party here. But I leave the dispensing of vengeance and recompense in the able hands of this wise jury, and Your Respectable Honor."

"I couldn't have said anything so good myself!" said Nate. "I rest my case. You can step down now, Mr. Grutt."

Rutherford was dislodging himself from the witness chair when Jess remarked, "Oh, there's just one other little matter, Nate. Mr. Grutt, if you'd kindly sit yourself down again, we'll see if the defense has anything to ask you."

"Gladly, sir," answered Rutherford.

Nate made another one of his objections, this one on the grounds that the simple and pure truth had already been told and any more talk would merely take the shine off the apple. Jess, however, was a man devoted to the proper appearances of these rituals and he invited Bernhard Klok to interrogate the witness.

At first, Bernie did not seem to understand that it was his turn to have a crack in the pulpit. Maybe he couldn't hear Jess over Clive's carpentry. Eventually, with the aid of gesture and shout, the judge prodded Bernie into the fray. He approached Rutherford and started talking to him, I guess. We jurymen could not hear a heard of it.

"Bernie! Speak up!" shouted Hal Steiner.

That seemed to confuse Bernie all the more, and he promptly shut up and sat down.

The trial might have settled into a stalemate if Jess had not ordered Clive to get himself a gratis drink, which inspired Nate to ask for another drink for himself. Jess ordered it done and for a time we were all spared the hammering and yammering of nails and objections.

When Bernie spoke again we could hear him well enough and often we actually understood what he was saying. "Mr. Grutt," he began. "Are you being today or ever, a miner?"

Rutherford leaned forward and inspected Bernie about the way you'd examine a two-headed calf. Then he raised his eyebrows, rolled his eyes, and asked, "Was that question in English?"

"He wants to know if you're a miner," explained Jess.

"My claim on Wet Wool Creek is duly filed and recorded. I got the papers right here if you want to see them," Rutherford answered.

"He says 'yes'," Jess translated. Then added, "You do mean 'yes', don't you?"

"Sure," Rutherford agreed. "I got the papers. I'm a miner."

Bernie then asked, "Mr. Grutt, what thing is 'gangue'?"

Rutherford sighed with gusto and looked toward Jess for assistance.

"He wants to know what gangue is," Jess prompted.

"Gan? Gan? Your Honor, what's this have to do with Harry jumping my claim?"

"Beats me," admitted Jess. "But do you know what gangue is?"

"Your Honor, as God is my witness, all I know is that Harry's a claim jumper and stole from me and probably was stealing from you too."

"The witness don't seem to know what gangue is. What's your next question, Bernie?"

"Mr. Grutt, in jumping, who and you saw Harry?" asked Bernie.

Rutherford was noticeably happy to be off the gangue problem and leaped into an answer. "I understand that question and I'm glad you asked it. On the morning of the twenty-fourth, the third time I saw Harry at it, Ephraim Kupperkeeper was with me. And Eph is prepared to testify to that fact as soon as he gets back from Pinoche."

By now, Nate had returned with his drink and chipped in, "That's correct, yer honor. Rutherford told me about Ephraim and I was going to bring it up later."

With not even a nod toward Nate, Bernie went right ahead with the queries. "Mr. Grutt, is a miner also, Mr. Kupperkeeper?"

"Oh, I get you now, Mr. Klok. Mr. Kupperkeeper happens to sell hand tools, but there's nothing wrong with his eyesight. And there's nothing wrong with his English, either. What else do you want to know? I'm not a man given to obfuscations."

Bernie ignored Rutherford and directly addressed Jess. "Herr Honor, can now Harry come talk?"

"Harry can testify if Nate don't have any more to say," said Jess.

"I got one question for Rutherford," Nate piped. "Did you see Lightload panning your claim, or not?"

In a resounding voice and with an evil squint at Bernie, Rutherford said, "I did!"

Next thing you know, Rutherford was back sitting with Nate who was triumphantly pounding him on the back, and Clive loudly returned to his task, and Jess was motioning Lightload in the direction of the Good Book, and we jury boys were fighting to keep awake in the mid-afternoon heat. Having more or less made up our minds on the Grutt versus Lightload case, we were now looking forward to stringing up L. B. Vail.

Nothing Harry had to say altered our judgment. It was pretty obvious that the befuddled orbit of the man's eyes was a fair reflection of the void within his head. Poor Lightload had the brains of a clingstone. Under Bernie's questioning Harry admitted that he was not at all sure what anybody was talking about, but he was mighty glad to see all his pals gathered in one place. Yes, he knew what gangue was. Didn't every honest miner? No, he had not done any claim jumping, although he did not hold anything against Rutherford B. Grutt, because he did not even know the sot, and had never seen him working a claim, period.

After Harry finished, Nate told the court that a fitting judgment would be the awardment of Lightload's claim to Mr. Grutt, even though Rutherford had been too civic-minded and modest to ask for it. Bernie greeted Nate's statement with a polite Teutonic guffaw.

Jess then admonished the jury against catnapping before it was time to render our verdicts. Otherwise, he would shut off the bar flow. This warning, plus Clive's hammering, plus the regular growls and chain rattles from L. B. Vail, kept most of us close to awake and we turned our consideration to horse thieving and murder.

The first witness against Vail was Merle Shank. Merle informed us that Vail and Bob Knox were first spotted loitering in the neighboring town of Pahranagat and the residents there were none too happy about it because no one liked the looks of the pair and there was no sign that these skunks had any visible means of support, unless it was desperadoing. Then Merle himself had spied Vail and Knox lurking in the hills east of Wet Wool Creek. Before a vigilante committee could look into the matter, half dozen horses, including Merle's white filly "Little Eva," had disappeared from Hiko.

The thieving varmints might have gotten away with it if God's hand and Vail's own intoxicated greed had not interceded. The morning after the theft, a pair of Indians brought a saddle into town to barter for corn meal. They claimed they had found it near the trail to St. George. Merle could identify the saddle as looking suspiciously like the one used by Bob Knox. A posse was quickly recruited and for a modest fee the Indians agreed to lead the men to the discovery point and follow the tracks from there.

That's all Merle could contribute because owing to the absence of Little Eva he was unable to join the posse. Jess asked Bernie if he had any questions for the witness. He did not. So then Clemson Howe was sworn in.

Clive's hammering and sawing were steady distractions while Merle spoke, and all through Clem's testimony, too. But at least I was now catching on to the purpose of the construction.

Clem told us that he headed up the posse, and from where the Indians had found the saddle, the tracks led as clear as a toll road five miles northeast toward Utah Territory. There the men found L. B. Vail encamped, unconscious in a drunken stupor atop freshly turned earth, and surrounded by eight horses. Six of the horses were the missing nags from Hiko, including Little Eva. One horse, the fattest one, was Vail's. And the remaining horse was the one last seen beneath the butt of the mysteriously absent Bob Knox.

After binding Vail with pulley rope, the vigilantes took to speculating about what lie beneath the soft dirt of his bedding. Upon digging it up they exhumed a human carcass. Despite the three slug holes in its head, the body was reasonably recognizable. Vail had been peacefully slumbering on the shallow grave of his former colleague! That's all Clem had to report and Nate observed that not much need be added.

The news proved pretty exciting to Clive whose sawing pace quickened to a frenzy. Vail, on the other hand, ceasing growling and rattling and took to silently branding Clem with fire hot eyes.

Bernie had only three questions for the witness. As best as I could understand them, they were:

Had anyone seen Vail steal the horses?

Clem answered, "No."

Had anyone seen Vail shoot Knox?

Clem answered, "No."

Did Clem have any idea why Bob Knox's saddle was found five miles away from the gravesite?

Clem answered, "Nope."

Jess let Clem return to the crowd, then told Bernie that if Vail wanted to say anything it was okay by the court. If Bernie wanted the jury to deliberate posthaste, that was also okay because the afternoon was wearing thin and Clive was nearly finished with his work.

Bernie said that Vail wanted a word or two, and the defendant dragged his chains to the witness chair. Vail didn't win any votes by answering, "Shit, yes," to the oath taking, but then he didn't lose any more either.

His story was simple. On the day before the horse thieving, he and Knox had an argument about a game of checkers. Vail contended that Knox cheated and Knox had claimed the opposite. They separated but Vail felt bad about the parting, they being life-long partners and all, so the next day he went looking for his old chum. When Vail found him a few miles up the St. George trail, Knox had six strange horses in his possession. Vail did not closely question the origins of the animals. He did, however, insist that in all fairness three of the beasts should now be his. This seems to have caused another disagreement and ultimately necessitated the plugging of old Bob.

It was unfortunate, Vail conceded. Still, the honest truth was that he had not stolen the horses and had only killed Bob Knox in self-defense. That's why he was innocently catching a little sleep when the posse found him, instead of lickitty-splitting toward Utah as any sensible guilty man would do.

Nate did not try to contradict Vail's testimony. He was only curious about why Vail slept on the grave.

"Because it was cooler there," Vail told him.

Bernie tried to get an explanation out of Vail about why Knox would abandon his saddle. Either the murdering thief did not comprehend his lawyer, or he couldn't conjure up a plausible lie. Vail claimed ignorance of any saddles.

That being the finish of all the legal maneuvering, Jess told us jurymen to get ourselves a drink and step outside to consider our verdicts. This we did.

It was pleasant to stretch my legs and the outdoors weren't as hot as the saloon. In less than the time it took to down our liquor, Hal Steiner gave his opinion of the two cases and asked all who agreed with him to raise their hands. We all raised our hands and soon went back to court for another drink and to share our unanimous wisdom with the multitude.

Clive Livingston was putting the final touches on his creation by smoothing its lid with a plane.

"Your honor," Hal said once we resumed our places. "The jury has decided. We got one question though. Are we supposed to hand out the punishments, or do you do that?"

Jess took on a puzzled look. "Let me get this straight, Hal. Are you asking if you boys personally must hang Vail?"

"No, we wouldn't mind that," Hal explained. "I mean, after we say he's guilty, who decides if we hang him or shoot him or tie him to a rock and let him rot in the desert?"

Enlightened on this point, Jess seemed gratified that the panel was taking such interest in the detail of the law. "Well, by tradition you boys give your verdict and can recommend any punishment you see fit. If it sounds good to me, I'll take your advice. Otherwise, I can come up with something better."

"Fair enough," Hal allowed. "The jury finds L. B. Vail guilty of horse thieving and he should be taken out and hung."

Vail turned his head and spit on the floor. Jess said, "So be it."

Hal paused in respect for the gravity of the judgment. Then said, "We also find that Rutherford B. Grutt is guilty of lying, and trying to use this court to cheat Harry Lightload out of his claim. We think it'd be fair if one of Rutherford's ears was lopped off to remind him to stay more honest in the future."

"That sounds reasonable to me," said Jess.

Rutherford blew off the ground like a first buggered pig. "Hold your horses here! I ain't the one on trial! You can't do that! Are you boys playing a joke on me? Don't I get a say?"

"You can decide which ear you'd miss the least," laughed Hal.

"This is an outrage!" Rutherford screamed. But everybody in the saloon was laughing so hard that I don't think his opinion made much impression.

"The court orders that these sentences be carried out before the sun goes down today," ruled Jess and he laid ballpeen to board with three conclusive thuds.

We took L. B. Vail out and hung him.

Then after much show of honing a cleaver to whack away one of Rutherford's ears, Jess suggested that true Nevada justice is often tempered with mercy. His Honor asked Hiko's citizens if the forfeiture of the Velvet Eldorado and Rutherford's immediate exodus from our fair community might be vengeance enough. We mostly agreed, and for recompense we sent half of the Eldorado south to Lightload Harry and the other half we sent north to Jess Samson.

Maybe The Lord could have done better. But the boys got their horses back. Hiko never again saw Rutherford B. Grutt. And Clive's box fit L .B. Vail just fine.

* * *

# Here Lies Busted Mac

I have always been fond of graveyards. As a little fellow back in Willimantic I often wandered the Shetucket Cemetery trying to decipher the markers and stealing the daisies when the opportunity offered itself. Nowadays I can read the epitaphs well enough but I usually leave the florals be. The experience, as a reminder that things could be worse, perks a man up if he is feeling gray. Then too, if a man is getting full of himself there is nothing like pondering a stone-cold crypt to underscore our mortal bond's only unbending proviso.

I am not going to get ghoulish on you. It is just when I think about Busted Mac I naturally think about graveyards and tombstones and the flowers in Shetucket Cemetery, and it's Busted Mac I'm aiming to tell you about.

His full Christian name was Robert Cornelius MacDougal. We did not know about the Cornelius moniker until it was too late to laugh about it. During his lifetime we called him "Busted" and I'll get to that part soon enough.

Mac came to Virginia City from Vermont sometime after The War and he was a stonemason by trade. To this day you can gaze at St. Mary of the Mountains in Virginia City and see plenty of Mac's work. Mostly though he did not cut stones for buildings because until the Great Fire of 1875 even the largest of Virginia City's structures were more likely built of wood. No, Busted Mac made a living carving gravestones, and back then business was brisk.

He had a fine way with a chisel and could make swirls and rose blossoms and chubby cherubs befitting the resting place of any rich old French king. Or he could cut stark and serious characters with C's and D's and M's and V's in the date so you could not tell when the fellow died and might think that here lies Pontius Pilate or maybe Pliny the Elder.

Everyone admired his artistry, but it was Mac's literary skills that truly elevated his work. The man could compose the pithiest epitaphs this side of the Old North Church. The fact that most of them were spurious skookum having little to do with the departed did not make them any less popular. Nor was the funeral crowd dismayed by Mac's admission that he lifted much of the verse from stones he had seen back in Montpelier. We liked the things, and whether staid or silly they always captured the note of quotable distinction that took some of the sting out of getting buried.

For Liam Murphy, a trout fancier, Mac carved:

> He angled many a purling brook,
> But lacked the angler's skill,
> He lied about the fish he took,
> And here he's lying still

For a dead dentist, he offered:

> Stranger! Approach this spot with gravity!
> Blaine Smith is filling his last cavity.

Rhyming was never a problem for Mac:

Here lies Simon Bun,
He was killed by a gun.
His name was not Bun but Wood,
But Wood would not rhyme with gun,
But Bun would.

A lot of the stones are still up there on Mt. Davidson for you to see for yourselves, but I imagine you can get the idea.

If you were to believe Mac's accounts, in the early days the most difficult aspect of his business was not dreaming up the final words or cutting them or even finding a suitable slab. No, the hardest thing was locating the cemetery. You see, back then the boys would isolate some reasonably level hunk of the mountain for a graveyard. Then they would plant a miner or two, but sooner or later a grave digger would hit what looked like a rich vein and the cemetery was forgotten in the rush to mid-wife the site into a new mine. Sometimes the previously buried coffins were moved. Sometimes the boys were a bit negligent on that account. After each of these false starts Mac and the undertaker had to scramble up a whole new resting ground and the process would repeat itself.

It was a trial for Mac, but even he had to admit they stumbled over a lot of rich ore in this manner and they never suffered from a shortage of ambitious volunteers to dig the graves. Eventually the corpses' luck turned to the better and Mac found a sticking spot that was not cluttered with great gobs of silver or gold.

Perhaps it was these speculative experiences with cemetery sites that prompted Mac to take up games of chance. Or maybe he was as eager as the next man to make a fortune without working too hard. I do not know. I can only say that by the time he and I began helling around together in '76, he was pouring all of his stonecutting earnings into poker and certificates of mine stock.

He was never without a fresh deck of cards in his pocket or a killing on the market in his dreams.

At the first our friendship maintained a predictable regularity that would have pleased a watchmaker. Mac would grab hold of me in the Whiskey Trust Saloon, tie his burly arm around my neck and say, "You dumb Yankee groundhog, is that cough getting any worse? Let me buy you a drink!"

I would be agreeable. Then, of course, courtesy required I buy the next two rounds, after which Mac would look over both shoulders to assure that no one was sharing our conversation and whisper, "Ya know, yesterday morning I bought twenty shares of the Silver Terrace Mine for three dollars per. In the afternoon the *Enterprise* printed that it was assayed at five hundred a ton and by evening I sold twelve shares of it for sixty-six dollars per. What do you think of that?"

I would think about it for a while, then say. "That's a profit of sixty-three dollars per and a net of ... "

"Seven hundred and fifty-six dollars!" he would almost shout. But nobody was much listening, so nobody much heard. "Trouble is, John McKissick blud me to death with thirty-fives in low ball last night and now I'm more or less busted."

"Ain't that the way it goes sometimes," I'd console.

"So here's what I'm going to do for you. I'm going to let you have five shares of the Terrace as collateral on a hundred dollar loan. So that's already a two hundred and thirty dollar profit for you if you want to settle for that. Or, if you want to wait until Thursday after next, I'll reclaim those shares for five hundred dollars and you can clear four hundred. Or, if you get anxious at anytime before then I'll just repay the loan with twenty-eight percent interest because somebody is sure to die tomorrow or my poker luck will change and I'll have some cash again. What do you say?"

Well, what would you say if presented with so many gilded possibilities from a trusted friend? I would loan him the hundred, when I had it.

Oh, I know what you are thinking. But you would be wrong. I always got my money back, eventually. And sometimes I'd even get a little more. Busted Mac was an honest man. That is why he always ended up busted. And that is why we called him that.

For the longest time his optimistic propensity to draw into inside straights, and his efforts to boodle into a bonanza for two bits a share, kept him on a steady diet of boom and bust. On the boom days he'd strut into the Whiskey Trust, set 'em up for the whole bottle-gang and say, "Remember boys, all of us are but squatters on this fruitful earth. But today I feel like a squatter in heaven!"

On the bust days, in addition to greasing the loan chute, he'd closely inquire as to the miners' health. Regarding funeral arrangements, he'd admonish us, "Remember boys, it's never too soon to be too late."

To me, his chosen confidant and easiest mark, he put on his *sotto voce* to share, "Better late than never. Fact is, the lates are best. The late Blaine Smith, the late Simon Wood ... all them late guys. I can't get enough of them."

I accepted such asides as I am sure they were intended ... little jokes of his profession meant to lighten the grievous duty of memorializing the departed.

All this biographical information about Mac has kept me from getting at what finally happened to him. I apologize to those of you still listening. To those of you asleep in the back row, I guess you are not interested in him anyways, so go on with what you are doing. You won't be missing anything worth laughing about. Busted Mac came to a sad end, and here is how he got there.

By the spring of '77, Mac had gotten half again smarter than when I first met him. He still thought a pair of queens could bluff home a seven-card pot, but he had moved out of the stock buying business. Now he was exclusively a stock seller. I won't bog us down again by explaining the difference in any detail. Just think to yourself: if you are always taking money in, and never putting money out, what would it do to your business? Of course, how Mac managed to obtain the stock in the first place without buying it is one of those tricks of the trade that always eludes the likes of you and me. So between carving tombstones and selling mine stocks, he more than made up for his hellishing bad luck at the poker table. Mac went up in the world, and he did it up brown.

He built himself a nice two-story brick home out at the end of C Street near Jim Flood's castle, and in the anticipation of someday taking a wife he had a piano shipped all the way from Toledo to put in the parlor. He donated his pewter spittoons to the Young America Volunteer Fire Company and placed silver ones in every room of his house. He bought a box at Piper's Opera and more often than not gave the tickets away to his customers. (The mine stock customers, not the tombstone ones.) He paid a dago tailor to travel from San Francisco to measure him up for six new suits and when they were constructed he engaged a freedman just to help him put the garments on and brush them off. And most fatefully, he hired four Chinamen to quarry and polish the tombstones. It was these Chinamen who broke the first spadeful of Mac's last hole.

Despite his rising status Mac did not put on airs. He would still set 'em up at the Trust and still borrow a sawbuck or two from me for old times sake and to let me know I was still his pal.

One day, Mac and I were sampling a newly arrived shipment of Dutch Gin when he dragged me into the back room and asked, "Have you ever heard of a fella named Fat Chance?"

I gave the question a fair amount of thought, because I have met more than my share of boys in the Comstock, and then answered, "Can't say as I have. Why do you ask?"

"Because I've heard he's the richest man in Nevada. Richer than a Midas ... and powerful. With agents not only in Nevada and California, but also in Mexico and Canada, and the Sandwich Islands, and all the way across the great Pacific to Shanghai."

"You'd think I might of heard of him," I said, but I was thinking if a wealthy man with a name as distinctive as Fat Chance existed anywhere, everybody would have heard of him. "Where's he live?"

"Right here in Virginia City!"

"Right here?" I asked, and I was skeptical because this was tough chewing. "You're telling me that somebody richer than O'Brien or Fair or MacKay or even Flood lives here and I ain't never even heard of him?"

"He's Chinese," Mac told me.

I took a swallow of the Dutch Gin and gave Mac a one-eyed squint that meant: Here is a good joke and I will listen to it, but don't you be thinking you've hit gullible gulch.

"My chink boys told me about him," said Mac.

"There's a reliable source," I encouraged. "A jabbering queue of heathen running around in nightclothes. What did they say?"

"Near as they made any sense, this Fat Chance is the chief mucky-muck of a big Tong."

"Tong?"

"It's like a Chinese Tammany Hall, I guess. The little bastards all kick in monthly dues that go into the pocket of this Fat Chance fellow. I don't know what they get in return, except if they don't pony up the coin they get a one-way ticket punched to ancestor land. How's that for a racket?"

I conceded that even for the pittance usually paid the Chinese, if somebody had enough of them in the club, the take might add up to a considerable pot.

"That's all real interesting," I told him. "But what's it have to do with us?"

"Not much to do with you, really, although I got a job in mind for you. But I'm thinking if I locate this bird he'd be a fool to pass up the chance to invest in some attractive silver futures I happen to have."

Not being an expert in fancy finance or foreign affairs, but being a little weary with the three dollars a day I was taking home at the time, I asked what seemed a reasonable question. "What do you want me to do, and what's in it for me?"

The sentiment met with Mac's approval. He smiled like a Congressman, "That's the spirit that built this country! I knew I could count on you. For now, just keep your mouth shut. But when I locate our friend, you are going to be my number one eunuch and bodyguard. I'll pay you a flat fee of thirty-five dollars per day of service ... or, thirteen percent of total profits. If I were you I'd go for the commission. I'm only doing this because you're just about the best buddy I have and anybody else would probably want a lot more money. What do you say?"

The money sounded good. Two details were troublesome. I was not overly enthusiastic about the notion of "bodyguard." It made me suspect there was more than one hole card in the deal. As to "eunuch"... I could not guess what a eunuch was or did. I expressed these concerns and, as usual, Busted Mac had a ready answer.

"You don't know the workings of the Oriental mind," he explained. "All the right Eastern bigshots got eunuchs and bodyguards. They're kinda like secretaries. And if I don't have at least one, I won't get in the man's front door."

"I won't have to carry a gun, will I?"

"Great heavens, no! This is legitimate business. Think of yourself more like a walking Masonic ring. I trot you along with me and you hand me papers when I want them, and this Fat Chance will know I'm in the same tribe he is."

"Okay, I'll do it," I agreed. Like I said, the money sounded good. We shook on the deal and I put it out of my mind because we took to seriously testing the palatability of Dutch Gin, and it was two weeks before Mac and I again crossed paths.

When we linked up after the fortnight, Mac was bubbly as shaken Champagne and he gushed a bucketful.

"I found him! Leastwise, I think I have. Tonight we make the rendezvous. This is auspicious, my friend, auspicious. A virgin field of possibility, like being alone in the mint. Wear something clean. Can you bow? I think we'd make a good impression if you bow a lot. With these Chinamen, the kow-towing business is all the rage."

"For fifty-five dollars a day I'll bow all you want," I ventured.

"Thirty-five," he corrected. "So you don't want the thirteen percent commission?"

"If it's all the same with you, I'll take my money up front and flat."

"Suit yourself, my friend. Get into your best duds and meet me at the Trust in an hour."

"Where's this Fat Chance live?"

"Uh, as to his exact place of business or domicile, that's still a shade hazy."

"Then where are we hooking up with this mogul?"

"That too, remains a little vague at the moment. We must expect some degree of inscrutability in this venture. But Soon Mee, one of my hired boys, assures me I have an appointment, and His Lordship is expecting us at nine tonight. So chop-chop. Business beckons."

I chop-chopped over to my boarding house and put on a clean shirt. Not versed in what the well-dressed eunuch was wearing that season, I refrained from more elaborate sartorial improvements and simply showed up as promised at the Trust. While awaiting there for Mac it occurred to me that meeting a fellow without knowing where we are meeting him is pushing the inscrutability a few degrees off the compass. Downright mysterious I called it. And as the hand played out, my call wasn't far off the mark.

When Mac arrived he was in the company of a shriveled bundle of somber coolie whom he identified as Soon Mee. The Chinamen I usually encountered, at the laundry and the barbershop and such, tended to be as obsequious as corset salesmen. Not Soon Mee. He was more of the dour sort with the same pained expression seen on the coolies who worked the borax flats at Columbia Marsh. Those fellows got their looks from toting hundred pound sacks in hundred-degree weather. I cannot say what weight Soon Mee labored under, but it must have been considerable.

"Soon Mee will guide us to Fat Chance," Mac told me.

"Fa Shan," said the Chinaman.

"That's right, Fat Chance. You leadee."

"Now. Go now!"

"Ain't he a pip?" said Mac. "He can't wait to get at it. I'll tell ya, I wish I had fifty more like him. They're gluttons for work these chinks."

After the V & T was built, the local Brotherhood of Silver and Gold Miners (they being fervently anti-gluttonous) had burned down the Chinese camp and chased most of them out of Storey County, but I did not think it polite to bring up old history with my present companions.

Mac handed me a leather portfolio stuffed with certificates of stock, ledger sheets filled with tiny numbers, and foolscaps with doggerel for future tombstones written on them.

"Here's your papers. I won't ever ask for anything specific. Now and then I'll just reach my hand back and you slap in the top thing on the stack. Got it?"

"Now. Go now!" insisted Soon Mee.

"Yes, we go soon, Soon."

To me, Mac added, "Don't forget to bow, you can't bow too much. And don't say anything, I'll do all the talking. And for God's sake, walk backwards when we leave him."

"Walk backwards?" I echoed, because I did not think I had heard him right.

"That's right. Like this." Mac demonstrated a backass shuffle complete with a riffle-full of kow-tows and smiles.

"If you say so," I said, and you are probably thinking Mac was a fool. Well, perhaps I should have thought so, too. Except maybe it is pretty shrewd to keep your eyes on some people when you are walking out the door with their money.

Mac said, "Okay. We're ready. You leadee now, Soon. Leadee to Fat Chance."

"Fa Shan," said the Chinaman and led us out of the Trust and into the night.

The little man seemed to know where he was going and was hell bent to get there. Mac and I were near a trot to keep up with him as he hustled along the V & T tracks past the Savage Mine in a southerly direction toward Gold Hill Town. At the Sutro Tunnel excavation he cut southeast and led us all the way down to the Quarry Mine where he turned southwest up to the Occidental Mine. From there we got on the Dayton Toll Road and went west through Gold Hill, crossed the V & T tracks again, and stopped at Crown Point Ravine in an alley between the Alpha Mine and a blacksmith's barn.

There he sat down on a rain barrel and lit his pipe.

"You lost?" asked Mac with some irritation.

"No loss," said Soon and peacefully puffed away.

"You leadee us to Fat Chance? You takee us now?" Mac tried.

"No go now. Go soon."

"But I want to go now!" Mac insisted.

"Go soon. Go soon," was all we could get out of him.

"The lazy bastard," Mac whispered to me. "You'd think I was paying him by the hour."

But Soon Mee was quite content to remain on his barrel until his bowl was exhausted. Mac and I were discussing if the methods of moving an obstinate mule would work equally well on a reposed Chinaman when Soon sprang up like a popjack and without a by-your-leave resumed his hurried pace now due north along the western perimeter of Virginia City. We chased behind, trailing in his dust by four or five yards.

Even with the help of a half moon, the backpath and gully route chosen by our guide gave Virginia City a slanted perspective and left me with an almost queasy disorientation. Still, I recognized the rear end of the Irving Mine when Soon made a sharp right turn and sailed east by southeast toward Flowery Ridge. Below the twin peaks on the Ridge he slowed his pace and approached a rickety one-room cabin that sat upon a fresh dig. This mine, if it was a mine, was a new one on me and I was wearing out some from the travel, so I was paying less attention to the terrain than I might have. Mac did not know exactly where we were either.

Soon stopped about a stone's throw away from the cabin and we could see a light burned from within it. I can say it was a stone's throw away because that is exactly what the Chinaman did. He picked up a small rock and hurled it at the structure. His line was true but he was short on distance. He tried it again and this time his rock skipped on one bounce and rattled against the door.

"If this is it, it doesn't look like much of a house for a rich man," I said.

"Hush!" Mac chided. "Can't you see we're getting the ol' initiation? They're lettin' us into the club, pal."

I accepted Mac's advice. No lodge or secret society had ever deemed me worthy of membership, so I was ignorant of these rites. The light from the cabin went out. Then Soon let us catch our breath, led us to the door, and entered. The place was dark as death. It had a dirt floor and no panes in the two windows. Other than that, I cannot tell you what was in it. For all I knew, a throng of Canton pirates was lurking in a corner.

I do not know how long we stood in there. It seemed plenty long. The Chinaman did not light his pipe or anything else.

Instead, he stared intently out an empty window frame. Mac did not say anything to Soon and I did not say anything to Mac. At first it was lighter on the outside than on the inside, so Mac and I joined Soon in looking for I-know-not-what.

Anybody who has been trapped in a winze after a cave-in knows how much you can hear when there is no sound and how much you see when you are blinded. When the moon dropped below Mt. Davidson the cabin became so quiet I heard the pirates slapping their cutlasses against their palms, and so dark I saw the gold rings dangling from their nostrils.

In the nonce before the cutthroats struck, Soon Me said, "Now we go Fa Shan."

Out the door he charged, working his skinny legs faster than ever. Mac and I followed at a run, which convinced me I was earning every penny of my thirty-five dollars. We were heading back into town. I knew this because the buildings we passed were getting crowded together. They were whizzing by so fast that I was not bothering to identify them. It was enough to watch the ground for the safety of my step and now and then eye Mac's pumping hind for my bearings. We shot through the God-only-knows cracks and crevices of Virginia City, cutting one way and another until I was dying for a drink but too exhausted to sniff out the fume trail of any near-at-hand saloons.

It was well past nine o'clock, so we had already missed the appointed meeting time. Initiation or no, I could see little point to this hell roaring rush.

Finally the damn Chinese rabbit came to rest behind a foul string of rough plank lean-tos footed by a drain ditch. Mac and I panted up to his side.

"I can't take much more," I gasped. "I worked today and I didn't bargain for this!"

Mac was breathing a storm and clutching his chest. Whatever answer he planned did not quite make it to his lips. He only bobbed his head and started mopping his neck with his handkerchief.

Soon Mee was no more winded than a man who had just rolled out of a bed. He calmly said, "Fa Shan here." And for the first time that night he smiled. Then he rapped an irregular tattoo on the door in front of us.

The dilapidated wigwam we stood behind was no more befitting a man of means than was the cabin by Flowery Ridge. At least this time the door was opened for us and we faced a chin-bearded Chinaman who, judging from his wrinkles, was three or four centuries old. The ancient nodded to Soon Mee and our guide wordlessly vanished into the darkness along the ditch.

At last getting some air into himself, Mac asked, "Mr. Chance? Are you Fat Chance? I'm MacDougal. Are you Mr. Chance?"

"Ma Doo Goo," replied the old man and he gestured us to follow him.

"Is this him?" I asked Mac.

Mac was annoyed with me. "I don't know! You just stay mum and let me do the talking."

The shack we entered was lit dimly with a few oil lamps. There was enough light to see it resembled a cross between an assay office and an apothecary. Wooden racks jammed the place floor to ceiling and on the racks were rows of bottles, some small and some bigger. Many of these containers held dusts and pebbles and stones of various colors. In other bottles were twigs and bark. In still others were dried flakes that looked like pot pourri, although they could not have smelled like it. The whole room had a malodorous reek of rotting carrion and sulfur water. The largest jars were truly frightening. Trapped within them, and immersed in a rust-hued liquid, were unidentifiable dead critters with claw-like beaks and slimy tentacles and little eyeballs popped out from their heads. Even if Chinamen were Christians, a place like this would give them a bad name.

Our taciturn pilot led us out of this maze into a much smaller room that must have been his living quarters because it had a bunk and table and pot bellied stove. He halted beside a large chest nestled against one wall. The thing was elaborately carved and lacquered and looked like it weighed a ton or two, but the old guy deftly slid it away from the wall. The pine board floor thus revealed looked like ordinary floor, yet he reached down and pulled open a trapdoor. Then he lit a candle in a holder and handed it to Mac.

"Ma Doo Goo, Fa Shan here," he said while pointing into the pit.

Mac lowered the candle into the chasm. The light revealed a ladder but I could not see any bottom to it.

"Much obliged," said Mac. To me, Mac said, "Ain't this some sport?"

I did not wish to dampen the game by giving my opinion. As I trailed Mac down the ladder I kept my eyes on the old Chinaman who silently closed the trap behind us.

It is a miner's instinct to count the rungs down a ladder. I counted sixteen before hitting ground. The candlelight sufficed for us to determine we were in a narrow and level drift shored haphazardly with timber ties of the old single-log style. This tipped me that whatever dig we were intruding had not been worked for a while. In a passage like this one, we modern miners would slap up double beam top-stops before even thinking about stepping down the line. Nevertheless, I stuck with Mac as he inched his way forward and I was wishing I had my work hat with head candle, and a few Pinkerton guards with brass knuckle-busters might be handy thing too.

Four or five rods along the way we came to an unsupported crosscut. Mac turned to me as if to inquire if we should look into it, but I shook my head no, and we kept to creeping along the straight path. That is when a light appeared from behind us. We jumped our heads over our shoulders and then jumped them back again when another light appeared from the tunnel's front.

The light from the front came closer and I saw it was a lantern attached to the hand of a coolie. The fellow approached us and raised his lamp to see our faces.

"Uh, howdy, friend," said Mac. "We're, uh, here to see Mr. Chance. But if we're in the wrong place, we'll just be on our way and … "

Mac stopped blabbering because the coolie leaned over and blew out our candle.

"Ma Doo Goo. Oh, yes. You good. You come, you come," beamed the coolie, and he bowed a few times while he shuffled backwards, pretty much the same way Mac had shown me back in the Whiskey Trust Saloon.

I could tell Mac was mightily relieved, as was I, for this was more like the treatment we expected from our Asiatics.

"Now we're getting somewhere," he said. "Lead on, my friend."

We followed our newfound pal into a wider passage with first-class boxframe shoring, which was a comfort. The light behind us tagged along at a discreet distance, and before long we came upon an iron vault-gate. With our approach an unseen hand raised the bars into the rock above and we entered what should have been a tool storage locker, only no tools were in evidence. It was filled with pale white smoke and lined with the bodies of dead Chinamen.

Whoa! You might be saying. "Whoa!" is what I said.

"Now don't let's get excited," were Mac's words.

Our usher had stepped over a few of the stiffs as if they were wet buffalo chips, while Mac and I stayed high and dry at the entrance.

Seeing our reluctance, the coolie said, "You come. You get Fa Shan. Fa Shan. Ma Doo Goo. You come." His grin revealed a mouthful of decayed tooth stumps.

"Well," said Mac after due consideration. "In for a dime, in for a dollar." And he waded into the pile with me clinging to his cuff because I sure as hell did not intend to be left behind at this particular juncture.

Once into the heap I noted with some surprise that the boys were not quite as dead as I first suspected. They apparently were in that state of saturated stupor of which I have known my share. Our trod through them prompted low moans and lazy scratching as we inadvertently stepped on a finger here or a nose there. The only difference between the multitude under foot and a typical miners' bummery was the absence of a rotgut aroma. True enough the dreaming Chinamen smelled of sweat and urine, but there was no hint of stale alcohol in the air. In an evening rife with mystery, this was a minor one.

On the far side of the chamber was a staircase similar to any you would have in your storm cellar. Up the stairs went the lantern and coolie, and faithfully up the stairs went Mac and I, leaving the bodies below to their slumbers. When we stepped through the door at the top we entered a hallway and the light near blinded me. I suppose the number of sconces on the walls was not greater than that illuminating the ballroom of the International Hotel, but after a night of increasing blackness the sudden effect of so much candlepower was like looking into the mid-day sun. Somehow our coolie slipped from ahead of us to behind and I felt his clammy hand in the small of my back gently pushing me through heavy curtains.

When our eyeballs adjusted themselves, Mac and I discovered ourselves in a room fit for a Sultan. It was large, as large as the Majestic Saloon on D Street. The floor was covered with a whole lot of tasseled rugs, all of which had patterns of strange animals on them. You could not see any solid floor because an uninterrupted carpet of woven dragons and whatnot extended from wall to wall. Except you could not see any solid walls either. More rugs, huge ones, hung on the room's sides and these had pictures of steep mountains or scenes depicting battles where the soldiers, Chinese I reckoned, were very small and the clouds above them were enormous. Without benefit of windows I could not tell if we were topland or underground. The ceiling offered no clue. It was a domed affair with deep blue tiles that sparkled with silver dust like stars in the winter sky. Hanging from it on golden chains was a score of wondrous lanterns, round as moons and fragile, and each was a different color but together they gave off an agreeable twilight. Divans set close to the wall-drapes ringed the space. Luscious soft things they were and plenty of them. We could have hauled up the inebriates from the basement and given them each a soft bunk and still have room for the stagger gang at the Whiskey Trust, so huge was this sanctum. The surrounding line of beddings was only broken on the far side by a metal standard which supported a pot. In the pot burned something that smelled like a fancy lady's perfume; the fragrance was sweet enough to make you think you could die happily in her arms. And plunk center of all of this were two facing chairs with legs carved like puma paws. The chairs were tucked on opposite sides of a round black ebony table whose surface reflected the silvery stars from the tiled ceiling. I knew we must still be in Nevada, but I could entertain the notion that we had dropped through a hole into China, or maybe into Paradise.

Mac said, "This must be the place."

And I said, "I guess so." Because it was nothing like I had ever drunk in, and the description I gave you hardly begins to give it justice.

I guess the little coolie had puffed out, although I did not see how. A body could not tell where egress or entrance existed, what with all the rugs obscuring the walls.

Mac and I were alone.

"Yep," said Mac. "I think we found him."

I said, "Well, let's have a sit, I'm run to a rag. I hope this Fat fella has a liquor stock."

No sooner had I made my dearest wish for the night when we heard the damndest bong sound. It was one hallow metallic note that shook through the air for a while, sort of like a bell toll, but it was not a bell, it was … Booooiiiiiiiiiiiiiinnnnnnnnggg! It sounded just like that.

Mac and I looked around us for where the sound emitted, could not figure it out, and when we returned our attention to the room's center, he was standing there — a slender Chinaman in flowing silk robe, tunic and skirt, and wearing spectacles. I had never before seen a Chinaman wearing spectacles.

"Good evening, gentleman," he addressed us. "Mr. MacDougal, I hope your journey did not prove too arduous."

"Oh, no. No. Nothing at all," said Mac. "Are you Mr. Chance?"

The man seemed wryly amused and answered, "Yes, I imagine that is the Anglican variation. Please, gentleman. Be seated." And he gestured toward the two chairs.

We took the seats and Mac pointed to me and said, "This here is my eunuch and bodyguard."

"Very appropriate," said Fat Chance. "I approve."

I gave the best bow I could from the chair. Mac gave me a big I-told-you-so wink.

There was not a chair left for Chance, so he stood while saying, "I am a great admirer of your poetry, Mr. MacDougal. 'Here lies the body of Michael Burke, Who lost his life while dodging work.' It has a terse eloquence that in my land is held in the highest esteem. If the first words fail, ten thousand will not then avail."

Like any artist, Mac was obviously pleased with this malarkey. "Why, thank you, Mr. Chance. I liked that one myself."

Chance proceeded to lay some more on.

"'Here lie the bones of Lazy Fred, Who wasted precious time in bed. Some plaster fell down on his head, And thanks be praised, Our Freddie's dead.' It's excellent ... a cautionary verse extolling the morality of industry and condemning the vice of sloth. You might be surprised as to the extent we Chinese share your Western values. Work fears the busy man."

"I'm sure it does," said Mac. "Are you a big one for epitaphs?"

"Unfortunately, I can only claim to be a dilettante. My interests are broad. Sadly, my expertise in any single subject, particularly the arts of America, is laughingly narrow."

"Oh, we can fix that up right enough, Mr. Chance. You seem like one smart customer. And your English is first-rate."

It was either all this oily back-slapping or the trip through the night air that made my cough hack up, and for the moment it interrupted the benedictions.

"You got to excuse my eunuch," Mac apologized. "He's spent too much time under rocks."

"I'd advise taking him to a physician," said Chance. "If unattended a cough such as that will only get worse, and you'll soon be in the market for a new eunuch."

Mac laughed like he had just heard the latest antic of the traveling salesman. But something about this Chance bird did not set quite right with me.

Mac got control of himself to say, "That's good advice, Mr. Chance, and I'll take it. But now I'd like to get down to business. I imagine you've heard I've got some sure-fire mining stock opportunities to offer you."

Chance held up one hand and from the look on his face you would think Mac had offered to bung out the man's latrine.

"I pray you indulge me, Mr. MacDougal. My home is not always easy to find and invariably my guests have come a great distance. You must be hungry and ... "

Chance looked directly at me.

"... thirsty. Please allow me to share a modest repast and refreshments. There can always be business in good time. An empty stomach makes empty promises."

This sounded like free grub and booze, and the prospect improved the man's standing in my eyes. I've made no secret that my throat was dry, made worse by the coughing, and I'll admit I was feeling a little peckish as well.

"Sure. Sure," Mac told him. "That's very neighborly of you. I could go for that."

"You honor me, sir, I assure you. A good neighbor is a found treasure."

With those words, two coolies emerged through a seam in the drapes carrying a monstrous velvet-cushioned highback chair and placed it under the fanny of our host. Another crew of coolies descended on us like gnats and set pretty porcelain plates and footed glass goblets on the table, while yet another bunch began relaying in bottles of hooch and platters of victuals.

If you are speculating that these supplies were the usual dump of Chinese garbage, you would be wrong as a mouthful of marbles. Heaped on the serving dishes were roasted venison steaks, fried pork chops, grilled swamp duck, bacon chunks, a boiled cow tongue, head cheese, an Iowa piglet ham, and beef ribs cooked in the Missouri fashion. Tucked between the meats were plates of hash fried potatoes, black-eyed beans, corn fritters, sugared crabapples, pickled eggs, blackberry muffins, stewed onions, buttered peas, sourdough bread, mullet cakes, and walnut rolls smothered with apple sauce. Anything else on the table escaped my notice, except for the dark ale the serving boys kept pouring into my goblet, and the ox-tail soup, and the mincemeat pie and the strap molasses pudding served for dessert.

It is an exhaustment just to tell you about it. Eating it all took concentrated effort, but Mac and I completed the job.

A meal of this proportion and quality might be available in San Francisco. More likely, you would need go to Chicago or, safer yet, New York City to find its like.

Our enjoyment was not lessened by the fact that Fat Chance did not eat a morsel. (Did I tell you Fat was not fat at all? He was normal to slim in frame.) Throughout the whole gorge he sipped tea from a cup with no handle and made small talk about the food. If I did not know better, I might have thought he had cooked the chow himself. Among other things, he told us the recipe used to cure the ham. He told us when to pick crabapples to avoid the bitterness. He told us how to gut Canadian geese; where wild onions were presently growing; which Sacramento merchants can procure walnuts; how long to properly boil a tongue; and you don't really need the tail to make good ox-tail soup.

After Mac and I shoved down the last scoop of pudding, Fat's minions cleared the bones from the battlefield and brought us brandy in tulip glasses. A box of Philadelphia cigars was offered all around and Mac lit one up.

Mac leaned back in his chair, started to put his boots up on the table, thought better of it, then said, "That was one hell of an eat, Fat." (Somewhere between the head cheese and the buttered peas Mac had cozied into a first name chumminess with Fat.)

"Mac," said Fat (for he had accepted the familiarity and returned it), "you flatter me. But the delicacy of the feast is the learned guest."

"Well said. And it's my good luck that I'm in a position to repay your generosity. Which brings us to our business. A smart man can make a bundle in mining stock, as I'm sure you know."

"Ah, yes," Fat agreed. "And the evening will not pass without negotiating an agreeable transaction. First, however, I would be negligent if I did not offer you an entertainment to aid your digestion. Are you a sporting man?"

In those days in Virginia City, "sport" meant one of only two things: easy women or hard gambling. By either measure Mac was one of the city's more dedicated sportsmen.

Cautiously, Mac answered, "I've been known to take my ... uh, that is, I ... yes. I am."

"Excellent. I suspected as much from the exquisite cut of your suit," responded Fat.

Mac beamed, for the dago haberdasher had billed him heavily for the duds.

Fat continued, "Perhaps you'd enjoy a game from my land, called Woa Na. It's a simple diversion, even children play it, but with the added interest of small wagers it's been known to amuse the most distinguished scholars."

Mac fidgeted in his chair a little. I could tell his stock options were burning a hole in his portfolio and the notion of gambling with a Chinaman, even one so gracious as Fat Chance, left him a mite uneasy.

"That's real white of you, Fat. But I don't want to take advantage of your hospitality. Maybe on some night when I have you up to my place."

"A good host fills the belly and the mind. It would honor me."

"Well ... " Mac wavered, "if it'd make you happy."

"Excellent!" smiled Fat, and immediately one of the houseboys set the game's paraphernalia on the table.

Right here I wanted to say something. The night had begun with a few pretty solid expectations and goals. Somehow we had made a couple bends off the road and now it was nearing midnight with us preparing to play Chinese faro, or heaven knows what exotic game, with a slick Oriental wheeler-dealer who was smugly awaiting the appearance of our money on the table.

Foolishly I remained silent. I remembered Mac's warning that eunuchs keep their mouth shut, and anyways, I might as well have been a lump of shag. The host and honored guest were not planning to deal me in.

As explained by Fat, the contest was simple, indeed. It was partly like craps and partly like the nursery game of pick-up-sticks. The "dice" consisted of twenty-seven short and flat wooden sticks. Twenty-six of the things were painted white on one side and black on the other. One stick was yellow on one side and red on the other. These sticks were placed in a leather frizzgig that looked like an oversized dice cup. The rules required alternating players to shake up the concoction and cast the sticks on the table. The betting was based upon how many sticks landed white face up and how many landed black face up. There were a few variations involving side bets on yellow and red, and you did not always have to use all the sticks in each toss, but none of it was too complicated. Craps is a better game, believe me. Bets were made with little blue shells. These functioned like poker chips, but were only half the size. Mac quickly got the gist of it and asked Fat how much a sporting man should buy in for. Fat said it did not matter. The real sport was in seeing the patterns made by the sticks. The money was only "dew on the flower's petal."

Mac bought in for fifty bucks worth of dew. For this he received fifty little blue shells and the game commenced.

They played for about an hour. Sometimes Fat won. Sometimes Mac won. Sometimes Fat won. Sometimes Mac lost. At the end of the hour all of Mac's little blue shells had snuck over to Fat's side of the table.

"Well," said Mac. "Busted again. But that was fun. Maybe I could return the favor by showing you how we Americans play poker."

"I'd be delighted," said Fat. "I am not completely unfamiliar with the game. Some Englishmen in Hong Kong taught me the rudiments. Please. Instruct me in the American version."

Mac's eyes lit up.

"Certainly. Certainly. My honor. Now this table is perfect. Round. Smooth. Couldn't be better. And those shells will make good enough chips. And I happen to have a deck with me, so we got a good start. Thing is, it's best if we have five boys in the game."

Fat clapped his hands and three of the servants came in with chairs and sat themselves at the table, happy as Indians at Thanksgiving. It was odd how that worked out so fast. Nobody asked if I wanted to play. I guess some eunuchs are in the club and some eunuchs are not.

Mac briefly explained the hierarchy of poker hands and the formalities of five stud. Fat translated this wisdom to his stooges. Everybody bought in for fifty little blue shells and the carnage began.

I am not saying Mac cheated the boys, no more than I would say that picking apples is cheating the tree. Fat could remember that three-of-a-kind beat two pair and aces beat kings and such, and he even started to get the hang of properly betting his hand. The rest of the gang could not distinguish jacks from queens, did not know a straight when they had one (although they caught on to flushes) and, best of all, bet the limit on every hand even when they had poop in the hole. In twenty minutes Mac had most of the shells, so the Chinamen bought more and Mac kept raking them in like Sally at the seashore.

As if their ignorance was not disadvantage enough, the whole bunch of them held their hole card out over the shiny black surface of the table. Mac always knew what they had from the reflection, and anytime he folded to a better hand he gave me another big wink.

All of this allowed Mac to be a solicitous winner. With sympathy for their rotten luck and with gentle instruction on the finer points of strategy he kept the pump flowing until four in the morning. When Fat finally put a cap on it by dismissing his three minions Mac had himself a gusher of little blue shells worth several hundred dollars.

"A fascinating game," Fat judged as he exchanged Mac's shells for greenbacks. "Perhaps when we play again I shall be a more worthy contestant."

"Oh, you played fine. Some nights the cards go one way and tonight I guess it was my way."

"Very true," said Fat. "Yet I think I have much to learn. Fishes see the worm, not the hook."

I was thinking the time might be ripe to make our farewells. Mac was tired too, I could tell.

Without his usual pep he said, "It's pretty late in the day, I know, but there's still … "

"Our business, of course. We shall do business, Mac. Would you understand if we saved that pleasure for our next encounter?"

"Sure. We can do that. It's late."

"If you would indulge me by sharing a pipe ... then my man will guide you home."

"Sure. I'd be happy to. You know, I never had such good luck at the poker table."

One of Fat's boys brought out a long skinny pipe with a small bowl. Fat lit it up, took a draw, and then handed it to Mac. Apparently when a Chinaman offers to share a pipe, he means it literally, sort of like Shawnee at a pow-wow. Mac sucked in some smoke then passed it to me. I declined. Owing to my cough I've had to give the stuff up. Although, even if I still indulged I have might have given it a pass. Chinese tobacco is a funny smelling thing and brought to mind the slugs down in the basement.

Between pipe passes Fat took to idly shaking the Woa Na sticks and spilling them on the table.

"We can tell fortunes with these. Did you know that?" he asked Mac.

"No," said Mac. "What do they say about me?"

Fat tossed the sticks on the table's surface and studied them. "They say," he smiled. "That Ma Doo Goo is going to be a very wealthy man and live forever."

"Hmmm," Mac purred. "That doesn't sound bad."

The two of them did not say much after that. They puffed away with their own thoughts and when the pipe was spent Fat rose and kindly thanked Mac for coming. Mac said he hoped they would get together again soon for business and sport because the evening had been enjoyable and enlightening.

Fat said, "Oxen plow the field, but the horses eat the grain."

Whatever he meant was left unexplained. Fat said goodnight and slipped through one of those drape cracks before I could even test a single kow-tow. The little guy who had brought us into the Grand Salon now appeared and led us out.

Our exit took a completely different route than our entrance. No more trampling over the bodies of delirious coolies for us. From the big room we parted through the drapes and descended thirty-nine steps down a steep iron staircase. We mazed our way through tunnels so narrow they required us to walk Indian-file and in ten minutes we found ourselves dumped somewhere along the Sutro excavation. Fat's little henchman surrendered his lantern to Mac while pointing up the line and saying, "You go. Safe go. Goodbye."

Mac and I followed the Sutro's main flush until we emerged at the tunnel's northwest mouth in the middle of the city. It was dawn. The streets were bustling with miners racing to beat the shift whistles and I was happy to return to the Occidental world.

Mac paid me my thirty-five dollars and said, "Well, I've got plenty to chew on. I'll let you know when we're going on the next expedition."

"Fine," I told him. "The grub's good. Only next time it will cost you fifty-five dollars because of all the exercise."

Instead of approving or denying my request, Mac added, "I'd sure appreciate it if you kept tonight's game to yourself."

"You got my word," I promised. I knew it would serve no good purpose to tell anyone about it. And besides, who would believe me?

We parted without further conversation. I returned to my boarding house to catch up on my sleep and Mac headed for his mansion on C Street presumably to plot another raid on the Oriental mint.

After our great adventure, however, Mac's visits to the Whiskey Trust became sporadic. On those occasions when he so honored us, he talked of this or that but made no mention of Fat Chance. Instead of frank discussion regarding stocks and loans, Mac became increasingly coy about his dealings.

That is a man's right and normally I would be the last fellow to push my nose into a friend's pocketbook. But curiosity eventually overcame my reticence and finally I asked him flat out, "Are you tapping Fat without my help?"

Mac squirmed some. "Oh, I see him now and again."

"Maybe I priced myself out of the market. I'll settle for thirty-five a night if you need my help."

"That's decent of you," Mac allowed. "And whenever I need a eunuch, you're my man. But things are smooth enough for the moment."

"Well, if business is going good for you ... "

I let the thought hang in the air, hoping Mac might share a few tips about making easy money.

He only said, "Profitable business is good. To sit and sip this glass is better."

This advice might have made more sense if Mac was drinking at the time. But his hands were empty and he seemed sober, so I could not make anything out of it at all.

If Busted Mac's own words left doubt about his fortunes, his actions spoke clearly about an ever-growing prosperity. Workers began construction on a new wing for his house, and in anticipation of acquiring a French mistress he had a pipe organ shipped all the way from Cincinnati to put in the conservatory. He donated his silver spittoons to the Young America Volunteer Fire Company and placed gold ones in every room of his home. He sponsored Adelina Patti to sing for eight performances at Piper's Opera House and held receptions in her honor every night for a week. He bought enough Wedgwood dishes and teacups to sit down sixty-four people at dinner and imported a real English butler to demonstrate the correct use of the utensils. And much to the regret of the dead and dying, Mac hired six more Chinamen and turned over most of his tombstone carving to them.

Such displays of obvious wealth did not escape the notice of Mac's old friends or the populace at large. Yet unlike the Floods or O'Briens whose every stock acquisition or mine sale was scrutinized at length in *The Territorial Enterprise*, the source of Mac's capital remained a mystery. No one admitted to buying stock from Mac. Inquiries at the Exchanges in either Virginia City or San Francisco would only elicit puzzled shrugs. We all knew stonemasonry alone could not account for such income. The bafflement was compounded because we ordinary folks stopped seeing Mac with the frequency of old. Even John

McKissick took to complaining that Mac's contributions to the weekly low ball game were sorely missed.

On those rare days when Mac brushed by us on the streets, his conversation favored profferings of unsolicited advice.

"Do not peddle wood in the forest or fish by the lake shore," he once counseled me.

Another time when I simply asked him where he had been keeping himself of late, he said, "Beat your drum inside the house to spare your neighbors."

Whatever his endeavors were, they must have been draining affairs. Mac's face was looking gaunt and those high priced tailored suits were starting to hang on him like gunny sacks on a stick. But to ask him if he was getting enough to eat would prompt a reply like, "Food cures hunger. Study cures ignorance."

More than a few of his old pals started speculating about his sanity. Still, nobody would say he was out and out crazy, not as long as his house on C Street kept growing and new luxuries from Europe kept arriving by the trainful.

As anyone with a brain might have predicted, the day came when the wind shifted.

It is hard to put a finger on any exact date. Rumor and gossip rarely etch in the details. The first thing we noticed was the erratic construction schedule on Mac's home. The laborers would get a day off here and there for no apparent reason. Then they would get rested for a week at a stretch. Unseasonable rain accounted for some of the inactivity, but not all of it. After a time, Mac told his crew that he was bringing in a new architect from Baltimore and work would stop until the man arrived.

The only catch was, months went by and no architect arrived from Baltimore or any place else.

Next, we heard Mac gave the boot to his English butler. This was soon followed by the release of his freedman. Then he let go eight of the ten Chinamen who were his hammer-gang in the tombstone business. When the word got around that Mac was selling his house, the boys at the Whiskey Trust sadly nodded their heads over their beer and said, "Mac's busted again, and gone crazy too."

I had to agree it looked like my friend's most recent squat in heaven was coming to an end. First-hand information, however, was sparse. We had not seen Mac for months. Nor had his pals at the Young America Volunteer Fire Company, nor had his swank chums at Piper's Opera House. No one could swear that Mac had left town. His stonecutting shop remained open, run by Soon Mee and another coolie, but no one could say with any certainty that Mac was still with us.

So I was surprised on the night when Soon Mee kow-towed up to me at The Trust and insisted that I follow him.

"Oh, no you don't," I told him. "I'm not following any more Chinamen for less than fifty-five dollars a roll. Nothing personal, it's just my well considered rule."

My statement made no dent on Soon.

"You come. Ma Doo Goo. You come," he persisted. "Ma Doo Goo want. Sick man."

"It's Mac? Where is he?" For now I was getting my curiosity up.

"You come."

I decided I could make an exception to my expressed policy as long as the coolie did not duck underground. I allowed him to lead the way.

The way led straight up C Street to Mac's house. Despite being a sometimes business associate of the man, I had never actually entered his famous home. My fantasies of a structure jammed to the rafters with tycoon-like opulence did not prepare me for what I saw.

Soon led me right through the front door into an entryway that was flat out empty. We proceeded to the hall that was equally devoid of furniture or knick-knacks. Curtains and drawn shades were on the windows but not so much as a footstool was inside. A glance into the dining room proved the gold spittoons, and the Wedgwood china, and everything else was gone. No pipe organ, no piano, no rug or picture frame graced the palace. As we stepped up the staircase the sound of my hobbed work-boots echoed off Mac's blank walls.

Soon opened a door off the landing and motioned me in. There, lying in a cheap old army cot with a wool blanket tucked to his chin, was Busted Mac — at least, what was left of him. His eye sockets and cheeks were hallow and dark. His frame was flesh painted on bone. The room stunk of sweat and urine. Because Mac was motionless and his lids were down I naturally took him for dead.

"He doesn't look so good," I said to Soon. The coolie said nothing and left the room.

Then the corpse opened his eyes and spoke.

"I've sold the house," Mac said.

"I heard that," I said. And asked, "Are you sick?"

"The white crane builds its nest from whispers," he informed me.

"You don't say. Have you seen a doctor?"

"Sold everything that was left."

"I can see that."

"I'm busted."

"I'm sorry to hear that. Do you want me to get you a drink or something?"

"With true friends, even water drunk together is sweet enough."

"You want some water?"

"The day your horse dies and your money's lost, your relatives turn to strangers."

"I didn't know you had any relatives."

"I don't have any."

"I didn't think so."

"All I have is peace and happiness."

"That's something, I guess."

"I'm wealthy."

"You mean healthy?"

"No, you numbskull. I mean wealthy."

The conversation was not following any of the well-trod paths familiar to me. It occurred to me that Mac was probably dying and had summoned me to his side for the exit. Under these circumstances anyone could be excused for mouthing all sorts of nonsense. There was no inviting place to sit down, so I shifted from one foot to another while I tried to imagine what words might comfort a man at the end of the track.

As if he could read my mind, Mac said, "I ain't dying."

"That's a comfort," I said. "Because to look at you I couldn't tell."

"There's a pipe under the cot. Get it for me."

I retrieved the instrument. It was the long stemmed type.

"Light it up for me," he ordered.

I could not see any harm in it, except to my own fragile lungs, so I did as commanded.

The pipe was filled with the vile Chinese stuff and Mac drew deeply of it.

"A man's life is a candle in the wind. A man's life is frost on the tiles," he told me.

"I guess so," I replied.

"I called you because I have a message."

"For me?"

"For everyone."

"Well, you know you can count on me. What is it?"

"Scholars talk books. Butchers talk pigs."

"That's the message?"

"No, you ninny. That's you. Which are you? A scholar or a butcher?"

Mac had me stumped with that question. While I thought it over, he went on talking.

"Before telling secrets on the road, look in the bushes."

"Is that your message?" I asked. As confused as I was, I still wanted to get the whole thing straight.

"Listen carefully," he instructed. "You can live forever. I am going to live forever. It is foretold. But first you must die. First, I must die."

I made a show of seriously considering his words, then said, "Is that what you want me to tell the boys?"

"That's it," he said.

"Okay," I agreed. "I'll tell 'em that, first chance I get."

"Also tell 'em that I am a happy, happy man."

"Sure. That too."

"You can go now."

In truth, I was happy to be dismissed. The discussion had lacked the light-hearted give-and-take that prompts a visitor to slip off his coat and stay a spell. Before departing I asked, "You sure there's nothing else I can do for you?"

"Yes," he conceded. "My pipe's gone out. Light it again."

I re-lit the pipe then got the hell out of there.

Dutifully I related Mac's words to anyone who would listen at the Trust. Everyone had a different notion about why Mac went bust and why Mac went insane. Most of the boys had personal experience in these matters and based their theories accordingly.

A rich divorced woman named Eilley Orrum moved into Mac's house a week later and she said there was no hint of the former owner's presence, not even a cot.

The last we heard from Mac came when Soon Mee and another coolie trudged into the Trust carrying a polished granite stone. They placed it on the floor and departed without further explanation. It was beautifully etched in Mac's distinctive style and read:

Here lies Busted Mac.
To know the road ahead,
Ask a man coming back.

✄

# ROBERT CORNELIUS MACDOUGAL
## 1831 -

A few of the boys helped me carry the rock up Mt. Davidson and prop it in the ground. We left the final date blank. Busted Mac was an honest man and we figured, when he was ready, he could carve it in for himself.

\* \* \*

## ABOUT THE AUTHOR

R.W. PINGER has worked as a playwright, theater executive, bartender, history and journalism teacher, and public school administrator. His plays have been produced by the Mark Taper Forum in Los Angeles, on National Public Radio's *Earplay* series, and by the University of California, Riverside. *Old Floyd Tells Tales* is his first collection of short stories. He resides in Eugene, Oregon, with his wife, the actress Rebecca Nachison.